Source of the River

Tales from Nōl'Deron

Lana Axe

AxeLord Publications
ISBN-10: 0692206094
ISBN-13: 978-0692206096
Cover art by Michael Gauss

For Laura.

"Water is the softest thing, yet it can
penetrate mountains and earth.
This shows clearly the principle of
softness overcoming hardness."
~Lao Tzu

Prologue

As he stood knee-deep in the water, Ryllak looked upon the lifeless form of his love. Her expression was serene, appearing as if she only slept. Fighting back tears, he reached out to touch her face. Before he could make contact with her skin, her body began to fade, disappearing within the blue of the river. No longer able to suppress the grief in his heart, Ryllak buried his face in his hands and wept. *Yillmara, my love, my all. How shall I go on without you?*

As he wept, his hatred rose for the one who had taken her life. "Curse you, treacherous creature!" he cried, staring into the water. "Show yourself before me!"

At his command, the Spirit of the river immediately seized Ryllak within a sphere of blue light. Stunned, Ryllak's body went rigid as he braced himself against an anticipated attack. No such attack occurred, though. Instead, Ryllak saw a vision of Yillmara in his mind, her blue eyes sparkling and full of life.

"Yillmara," he whispered.

It was not her voice but another who replied, filling his mind with these words: *Your life-mate has chosen this path. She has traded her life for that of her child.*

"Curse you for making such a trade. You are a creature of evil."

I have granted a life as was asked of me.

Ryllak's mind thought back to the stillborn child his life-mate had brought to the river. She had desired nothing more from life than to be a mother, and her heart had been broken by the news that her child did not live. In his grief for Yillmara, Ryllak had not even looked upon their child, the child who Yillmara had died to save.

The Spirit spoke no more, and Ryllak was released from the blue light. Tears still fresh upon his cheeks, he returned slowly to the riverbank. Glancing once over his shoulder in hopes of seeing his love, he beheld only the reflection of the early-morning light as it danced upon the water. His heart heavy, he proceeded back to his home.

Once inside, he saw his son in the arms of a nursemaid. Silently, he stared for a moment, trying to gather his courage. This child had cost him his life-mate, but he felt no animosity toward him. This tiny creature had not asked to be born, and he would have brought immense joy into Yillmara's life.

Slowly, he approached the nurse and stretched out his arms to take the child. With a soft smile, the nurse handed the child to his father.

"He's a beautiful boy," she stated, her face beaming.

Ryllak looked down upon the child and into his sapphire-blue eyes. The child did not cry nor make any other sound. Although he was too tiny to speak, the child's expression seemed to be telling Ryllak that all would be well. Tears filled Ryllak's eyes as he clutched his newborn son to his heart and kissed his forehead.

"I am your father, and I will love you until the world has come to an end," he declared.

The baby cooed softly, resting peacefully in his father's arms. The Spirit of the river had granted his life, and much would be expected in return.

Chapter 1

Ryllak paced impatiently as he waited for his son to return home. The grass in front of the large silver tree was beginning to show signs of wear as he quickly stepped back and forth. After a while, he stopped pacing and leaned his back against the tree. The spring air was cool, and the afternoon sun hid its face behind a thin layer of clouds. He could not, however, enjoy the fine weather. He feared his nerves might get the better of him when he finally told his son the truth.

Finally, River appeared in the distance carrying a small stack of books beneath one arm. His cousin and closest friend, Galen, accompanied him. Ryllak watched and waited as the young elves made their way across the village. They were both tall and slender with long dark hair, and might have been mistaken for brothers had it not been for River's sapphire-blue eyes. Those eyes singled him out every time as someone special among the Westerling Elves. Blue eyes were not rare, but River's particular sapphire hue had never been seen before in the Vale.

As the two approached, Ryllak stood up straight and crossed his arms. His face was stern, and his brown eyes stared intently at his son.

"Is everything all right?" River asked, noticing his father's serious demeanor.

"We need to speak," Ryllak replied.

"I think it's time for me to go," Galen said. He gave River a slight shrug and raised his eyebrows as he turned to walk away. "Good luck, River," he added quietly.

River followed his father inside the arched doorway of the silver tree. Inside was a spacious home that was impossibly larger than the tree that held it. The magic of the forest supplied homes to the elves that did not require damaging any of the trees. The elves and the woods lived in harmony, each gladly accommodating the other.

"Sit down, Son," Ryllak said.

He took a seat on the cushioned bench of the great room and patted the seat next to him. River sat, but

Ryllak remained silent. He stared out the window overlooking the gardens, lost in thought. Finally he realized he could delay no longer.

"Son," he began, "in two days' time, you will be two hundred years old, and you will come of age. You will no longer be considered a child to us, and you must take your place among our people."

River's eyes darted around the room as he searched his mind for a response. He knew he was coming of age and would be expected to take on adult responsibilities. He hoped to leave his father's home and begin his own life, but deciding what to do with a life of thousands of years was no easy task for a young elf. Failing to find the right words, he remained silent.

Ryllak sighed deeply and said, "I have told you of your mother and how she died in childbirth, but there are other things I haven't told you."

River, who had been staring at the floor, looked up at his father and stared into his eyes. He could tell what his father was about to say was serious, and it was difficult for him to say it.

"What is it, Father?" he asked after a few moments of silence.

Ryllak looked away from his son and said, "Your mother was taken by the river. You were stillborn, and she traded her life for yours."

River was stunned by this news. Stumbling in his words, he asked, "How? How is such a thing possible?"

Ryllak cleared his throat and replied, "The Spirit of the river granted your life. We tried for many years to start a family, but we never had any success until Yillmara prayed to the river for a child. That is when you came to us, and the Spirit took her away."

River's eyes filled with tears for his mother, who had given up everything for him. Her selfless love overwhelmed him, and he was unsure how he should react. He had heard many stories of her and her sweet nature, and he regretted not having the chance to know her. His father had always been good to him, but not having a mother to turn to had been difficult.

"I do not know the Spirit who dwells in the river," Ryllak said. "It has always been there, and it protects our people. I believe its intentions are good, and Yillmara was most willing to trade her life for yours. Do not feel guilty that you are here and she is not. She loved you more than words can describe."

"But the Spirit killed her," River replied. "Surely that was unnecessary."

"It takes a Spirit of immense magical power to create a life. To grant an elven life, it must have another life freely given. That is the only way to maintain balance."

"Then I owe my life to this Spirit," River commented.

"In more ways than one," Ryllak said. "Your mother became pregnant immediately after praying to the river. I have loved you and raised you as my own, but I believe the Spirit is your true father."

A look of realization spread over River's face. All his life he had felt compelled to visit the Blue River and stand at the base of the waterfall. He would stare into the flowing current for hours and release his mind from all thoughts but water. As he neared his coming of age, the compulsion had grown stronger. He had visited the river daily for the past few years and felt an unknown presence around him.

"This is why the Elders have always looked at me strangely," he said. "I thought I was imagining it, but they already knew all of this. They knew I was not an ordinary elf. I'm some sort of magical hybrid. What am I, Father?" He stared at his father hoping for an answer.

After a few silent moments, Ryllak said, "You must ask that question of the Spirit. Perhaps you will find the answers you seek within the river."

River sat motionless for a while. The younger elves had always treated him as one of their own. All of his life he had excelled at water magic, and he had simply considered himself talented. All elves were born with magical abilities, but his heightened abilities would now be attributed to his origin as a creature of magic. He had no desire to be different from the other elves, but it seemed he had little choice in the matter.

The Elders had always seemed suspicious of him throughout the course of his magical studies. He had felt singled out from his fellow students on many occasions. Frequently, his professors would require him to explain exactly how he had performed a task as simple as watering an herb garden. No one else was ever required to explain himself, but he had been questioned and interviewed by members of the Elder Council several times. Once, during a heavy rain, he was asked to stand beneath the drops and count them. At the time he thought it was some sort of punishment, but he had broken no rules. Now it was beginning to make sense.

After a while, he decided to pay the river a visit. He saw no harm in it and hoped he might find some answers there. As he walked through the village, he glanced around, wondering if anyone saw him differently. Of course they had not been present to hear his father's words, but he could not help thinking that everyone would know the truth of his birth.

As he reached the bank, he removed his shoes and waded down into the water. It was cool, and a soft breeze wafted gently across its surface. The smooth rocks along the bottom provided a finely crafted natural floor. He made his way toward the waterfall, where the river tumbles down from its source in the mountains. The sound of the roaring water drowned all the noise of the village and the sounds of the forest.

Standing in front of the rushing water, he gazed into the foam, which floated lazily away from the falls. The sights and sounds of the water had a hypnotic effect on him, and his mind began to drift. He entered a state of calmness and surrendered his mind to the river.

A blue, swirling mist formed around his waist. The light grew larger until he was completely encompassed by a wave of blue magic. He welcomed the sensation, closing his eyes and lifting his arms above his head. The Spirit had come. River could hear its voice within his mind.

Child of the river, your spirit has awakened. Within you dwells the soul of the water, your true form. This blessing I have given you, and in time, you must return it. Each day you will visit here at dawn, and I will show you your path and lead you on your journey.

Who are you? River projected with his mind.

I am the Spirit, the Soul, and the Heart.

With those words, the voice went silent, and the blue magic faded away. As he turned to face the village, he noticed that many of the Vale's citizens had gathered at the bank to see what was happening. His father was among them.

Slowly, he made his way back to the bank. As he stepped onto the sand, his long hair, which was previously dripping with water, became immediately dry. His long gray robe was dry as well. A few of the elves stepped away from him, some of them gasping.

His father strode forward and wrapped an arm around his shoulders, guiding him away from the bank. He led him back to their home and asked, "Did you find what you needed?"

"I think so," River replied. "There are many things I need to learn. The Spirit in the water is going to teach me."

Ryllak nodded and patted his son's shoulder. He knew River would change when he came of age, but he had no idea how much. A bright future awaited him, that much was certain. He would be there to help in any way a father could.

Chapter 2

River awoke before sunrise, and his mind was troubled. Though it had been more than a month since his father informed him of his true paternity, he could still remember every detail. The revelation had changed his outlook on life, and he was determined to live up to the destiny he had been given.

He still regretted never knowing his mother, and he wished he could speak with her at least once. On several occasions, he had asked the Spirit if such a thing were possible. The Spirit always responded vaguely, and River was never sure how to interpret the response. A few times, River thought he had seen his mother's face amid the waters. It was only ever a glimpse, and he was never certain of what he saw.

He rose from his bed and proceeded toward the riverbank. As always, the first thing he did in the morning was visit the Spirit and bathe in the waters of the river. He would offer his life back to the Spirit who had given it, submitting himself to its will.

The Spirit had taught him many things over the past few weeks, and River had resolved to make himself useful to the elves of the Vale. Some of their distrust and uneasiness had disappeared as he was growing up, but some of the Elders still had their concerns. Creatures of magic were not fully understood by the Westerling Elves, but they were generally accepted as long as they were good-natured. The magical creatures of malevolent design were kept at bay by the magic of the forest. Their kind were not welcome in the Vale, and no elf sought them out.

River was of an unknown magical design. Though the River Spirit had never caused harm to any other elf in the Vale, Yillmara's death had made them all uneasy. What had once been a helpful and pleasant creature was now suspected of murder. That suspicion did not easily leave the Elders' minds. Their reservations about River and the water spirit within him seemed justified. Any creature who could command such power over life and death deserved to be monitored closely.

River himself had a good heart, and his only desire was to be of help to his kinsmen. Recently he had used his newfound powers to bring rain as needed and ensure the safety of the Vale by placing magical barriers at its borders. No one with evil intent could ever cross the river to enter the Vale as long as River lived.

The air outside was fresh and cool, the birds sang merrily overhead. A gentle breeze caressed his skin as he removed his silver robe and entered the cool water of the Blue River. His dark hair trailed freely behind him, floating at the water's surface as he swam to the base of the waterfall. Nearly five hundred feet in height, the waterfall deposited the remains of snow melting high up in the Wrathful Mountains. At its base were large charcoal-gray boulders, which were suitable for sitting and spending a peaceful afternoon. Near these boulders, River would commune with the Spirit and seek its guidance.

The water was surprisingly warm, considering its source. Weather in the Vale brought a permanence of springtime for the Westerling Elves to enjoy. There were still rainy days to contend with, but the rains brought new life to the forests and provided sustenance for the creatures within.

As River reached the base of the waterfall, an uneasy feeling came over him. He tried his best to shake off the feeling and concentrate, but he found it impossible to focus his mind. Taking a few deep breaths, he proceeded to wash himself in the clear blue waters. After a few moments, he noticed movement from the corner of his eye. High overhead, an object was falling from the top of the waterfall. River stared at the object, his mouth dropping open. Within a few seconds, it hit the water, crashing violently below the surface.

Glancing overhead to be sure a second item wouldn't follow the first, River moved toward the fallen object. As he moved closer, he could plainly see that this was not some random bit of debris. A dwarf had fallen to his death from somewhere in the mountains.

Nervously, River approached the dwarf and looked down on his lifeless form. Placing a hand at the side of the dwarf's neck, River could feel no trace of a pulse. The dwarf's face was pale, suggesting he may have been dead before the fall. There were no obvious bruises or cuts on his skin, which seemed strange considering the route the body had traveled to reach the Vale.

Others within the village had witnessed the spectacle and were on their way to investigate. A few of them had already gathered on the bank, watching intently as River inspected the corpse. Ryllak noticed the commotion and decided to make sure River was all right.

Pushing his way past the crowd, Ryllak waded into the water and made his way to his son's side. River's face was troubled, and Ryllak reached out to comfort him.

"Are you all right?" he asked.

"Yes, but this dwarf certainly isn't." His concern was obvious in his voice, his hands shaking slightly as he placed them on each side of the dwarf's head. Blue magic spread over the body as River looked inside the dwarf's mind.

Ryllak waited anxiously, maintaining his silence so as not to break River's concentration. He worried what his son might see and hoped it would not be too much for him to handle. Though he was of age, Ryllak could not stop thinking of him as a child.

"This man was ill," River said softly. "He is a miner from a dwarf village in the mountains, and he became ill shortly after beginning his work this morning. He went to a creek somewhere above to cool his fevered skin before falling in." River removed his hands from the dwarf and looked at his father. "I believe he drowned and was carried away for miles in the current before ending up here."

Thinking of his son's welfare first, Ryllak replied, "Is this illness contagious? Should you be touching him?"

"I don't know what it is," River admitted. "The Spirit may know since the dwarf is in its waters. I don't sense any danger for myself, but for the rest of our village I cannot say."

"You should speak to the Spirit, then," Ryllak said. "I will move this unfortunate dwarf to the riverbank." Carefully, Ryllak dragged the body away. As he reached the bank, other elves offered their assistance in pulling the dwarf from the water.

River turned his attention back to the waterfall and stared into the deep blue water at its base. Focusing his energy, his eyes flashed sparkling blue. The Spirit had come to offer its guidance. Sensing its presence, River relaxed his body, allowing his mind to open and receive the Spirit's words.

Ryllak gazed out into the water where River stood encompassed by a pale-blue light. He hoped the information his son received would be good news, but in his heart, he knew that would not be the case. The appearance of this dwarf was far too strange to be a mere coincidence. Such a thing had never before occurred in the Vale.

Patiently he waited until River began making his way to the riverbank. As he drew closer, Ryllak could see the concerned look on his son's face, and his heart sank. There was trouble ahead, and he feared that his son might soon be in grave danger.

Chapter 3

Thunder rumbled softly in the distance as Kaiya sat motionless, her face turned toward the wind. A gentle mist began to fall, and she lifted the hood of her gray woolen cloak. The sky grew ever darker, encompassing the dwarven villages of the Wrathful Mountains in shadow.

"You'll catch your death out there!" Kassie cried, leaning her head out of the doorway. She promptly slammed the door shut to keep out the rain.

"Coming, Mum," Kaiya replied quietly. Slowly, she stood and made her way back to the farmhouse. Only once did she pause, gazing one last time at the sky. Taking a deep breath, she filled her lungs with the fresh scent of rain that precedes a storm. With a sigh, she continued inside her home.

"There you are," her mother remarked.

Kaiya removed her damp cloak and carefully placed it on a hook near the door. "It's not a bad storm," she said. "There's no need for a fuss."

Kassie giggled with joy as she looked upon her daughter. "You're all frizzy from the rain, my dear." Licking her hand, she attempted to smooth Kaiya's short violet locks.

"Stop, Mum," Kaiya said, backing away. "It's fine."

"Of course it is," Darvil broke in. "It's not as if she's after a husband."

"Not tonight, anyway," her mother replied with a smirk.

"If you're going to remain an old maid, at least help your mother with dinner," he grumbled, scratching the thick red beard on his chin. "It's not right to still be living with your parents at your age. It's high time—"

"I found a husband and got on with my life— yadda, yadda, yadda," Kaiya finished.

"It's that smart mouth of yours that keeps you from finding a man," her father declared.

Sighing, Kaiya joined her mother in the kitchen.

"Don't listen to him," Kassie said. "He's glad to have you here to help out, even if he doesn't want to admit it. The boys have gone, and my sweet girl can stay as long as she likes." She smiled warmly at Kaiya.

"I still wish he wouldn't say things like that," she replied. "It's already hard enough being different."

"You're special, that's all," her mother said. "Someday you'll find someone who's right for you, and then you'll be off to have children of your own."

Kaiya did not reply. Having children was not on her list of things she wanted to do. All her life she had been treated as an outcast, thanks to her magical abilities. Dwarves were not known to possess such skill, and none of her peers could relate to her situation. She was different, and that was all the reason they needed to be cruel. Her father's constant reminders of her lack of a husband did not help matters. At nearly thirty years of age, she was already older than most brides. Marriage did not matter to Kaiya. She had dedicated every free moment to the study of magic, and she did not intend to suppress her talents in order to fit in.

Outside, the wind started to howl. Kaiya dashed to the window to look upon the storm. The trees danced and swayed, urged on by the powerful gusts. Lightning reflected in her gray eyes, and she felt a sudden surge of power rush through her body.

"Come away from the window, Kaiya," her mother said softly.

Kaiya did not reply. Instead, she remained silent, entranced as she looked upon the storm.

"Kaiya," her mother said again. "Please."

Dropping her gaze to the floor, Kaiya moved away from the window and took a seat at her mother's side. "I sense a presence in the storm," she said quietly.

"You're scaring me, Kaiya," Kassie replied nervously. "Let's just have dinner, all right?"

Still troubled by the feeling, Kaiya nodded and rose from her seat. Retrieving dishes from the cabinet, she suddenly felt sick to her stomach. An intense headache overcame her, and she dropped her head into her hands.

"Kaiya, what is it?" her mother asked, concerned. Rushing to her daughter's side, she helped her back to her seat. "Tell me," she said.

"I don't know," Kaiya replied. "I feel sick all of a sudden. There's something out there, Mum. I don't think it's something nice."

Darvil made his way into the kitchen hoping to eat but saw that his daughter was ailing. "What is it, girl?" he asked as tenderly as he could manage.

"She's not feeling well," Kassie replied. "It's that magic. She senses something in the storm."

"An evil spirit?" Darvil asked. "That's the only thing that could account for this." He bent forward and patted his daughter's head. "Let Papa help you to bed," he said, helping her to her feet.

Kaiya nodded slowly and rested her head on her father's shoulder. Together they ascended the stairs to Kaiya's room.

After helping her into bed, Darvil said, "You know I love you, girl. I didn't mean those things I said about having you married off."

Weakly, Kaiya replied, "I know, Papa." The pain in her head intensified, and tears filled her eyes.

Kassie made her way up the stairs with a bowl of cool water and a cloth for Kaiya's forehead. Gently, she patted her daughter's face with the damp cloth, hoping to soothe her pain. The storm continued to rage outside, and the wind howled as if crying out for help.

With a sudden jolt, Kaiya bolted upright in her bed. Kassie jumped back, startled.

"What is it?"

"The wind," Kaiya replied, her gray eyes beginning to shine with magic. "It's calling to me."

"Let it call," Darvil replied. "You need your rest." He quickly went over to the window and fastened the shutters.

"Rest, dear," Kassie said softly, still patting Kaiya's face with the cloth.

Kaiya settled back into her bed, squeezing her eyes shut. *Just breathe*, she thought. *This will pass.* The wind continued to call, and she fought the urge to run out into the storm. She knew there was no danger for her, but she did not wish to frighten her parents.

Somewhere nearby, a presence had awakened. Though she did not know exactly what it was, Kaiya knew it was evil by nature. A dark spirit had come into the Wrathful Mountains, and its purpose was unclear.

Despite the evil presence, Kaiya felt no fear. With the wind as her ally, she knew she would be safe from harm. Her family, though, might not be so lucky. Danger was about to descend upon the dwarves of the mountain.

Chapter 4

Telorithan took a seat in his former master's library to await his arrival. He smoothed out the wrinkles in his long red robe and casually twirled a silver strand of hair on his finger. The mirror above the fireplace attracted his attention, giving him yet another opportunity to admire himself. *There could never be another as beautiful as me,* he thought. His blue eyes sparkled, accentuated by the bronze-toned skin of his face. *I am truly perfection.*

Though he had been sitting only a few minutes, he began to tap his finger against the arm of his chair. Patience was not a virtue he possessed. When he wanted something, he wanted it immediately, and nothing could stand in his way. Today he came seeking his mentor's advice in hopes that the old elf would be able to assist in his latest endeavor.

Finally, Yiranor entered the library wearing his usual red-black robe, his face showing his advanced age. He smiled warmly at his former apprentice. "So delightful to see you, Telorithan. It's always a pleasure to have you visit."

Remaining in his seat, Telorithan nodded. "Yes," he replied dismissively. "Tell me, do you have any knowledge of the process of soul binding?"

Yiranor was momentarily shocked by the question, his mouth dropping open in reply. Telorithan raised his eyebrows, awaiting a response. Slowly, Yiranor regained his composure and took a seat opposite his guest.

"It's a banned practice. Please tell me you aren't wasting your talents on such nonsense." His dark eyes regarded his former pupil suspiciously.

"Always the teacher," Telorithan replied, shaking his head. "As a matter of fact, I have been doing some research in that field. I have had success with animal specimens, and I'm planning to expand my research to include elven subjects."

Yiranor, who was taking a sip of tea, coughed and sputtered. Telorithan sat unmoving and expressionless. The practice of soul binding had been banned for centuries in the Sunswept Isles. No

34

Enlightened Elf had publicly admitted to performing such magic in living memory.

"I am shocked by this, Telorithan," Yiranor finally replied. "You were among the youngest ever to achieve the rank of Master. You were the finest pupil I ever taught, and now you are wasting your talents on this? Is this what you've been doing for the past two hundred years? Tell me I have misunderstood."

"On the contrary," Telorithan said. "You have understood me perfectly. It is my intention to eventually bind the essence of a god."

The old elf stared at him in disbelief. "The gods cannot be bound. That is what makes them gods."

"Yes, but they were elves once," Telorithan replied, his voice becoming excited. "No one has discovered what process they used to make themselves what they are now. I have searched high and low, finding nothing but dead ends. With soul binding, I don't need to know their process. I can simply take what they already have."

"Simply?" Yiranor echoed, jumping to his feet. "This is no simple task you speak of. Soul binding takes immense concentration and vast amounts of power."

A wicked grin spread across Telorithan's face. "So you do have some knowledge of the process?"

Sighing, Yiranor sank back into his chair. "I admit I have studied such things in the past. I was intrigued by the process, but I never practiced it on any living creature."

"What exactly did you study? Where can I find more information?" Telorithan leaned in close to Yiranor, interlacing his fingers in an effort to stop himself from fidgeting with excitement.

"We should not be speaking of such things." Yiranor was plainly uncomfortable with the conversation.

"But we are speaking of it," Telorithan replied. "Why is the process banned? Because other sorcerers did not have the power to control the bound essences. They were failures. I *will* succeed."

Yiranor eyed him suspiciously, still unsure if he should share the information he was withholding. Telorithan had been an extremely talented student, but he could be impulsive and was quick to anger.

Seeing that Yiranor was not yet convinced, Telorithan tried again. "If I can perfect the process, everyone will want to perform this magic. The process will no longer be banned." These words were empty.

Telorithan had no intention of sharing anything he had learned or was yet to learn with any other sorcerer.

Considering his former student's words carefully, Yiranor asked, "Do you truly think soul binding could be put to good use? Which elves would be subject to the binding? How would you choose?"

"We can use criminals for practice. Once the process is perfected, anyone is fair game. If you don't want your essence bound, you had better be strong enough to put up a fight."

"That's a dreadful way of putting it, Telorithan. I hope you didn't expect to convince me with such talk." Yiranor had always been somewhat frightened of his apprentice, but he tried not to show it as he spoke.

"Honestly," Telorithan began, "I am doing this for my own benefit. If others wish to follow along afterward, it is no concern of mine. No one is as skilled as I am. No one else will be able to bind a god." He did not bother to hide his conceit. To him, the only thing that mattered was obtaining his mentor's help. Somewhere within this library was a scroll that could answer all of his questions. He was determined to obtain it at any cost.

"I suppose that is for the best," Yiranor admitted. "I do not relish the thought of elves dueling over trivial matters in an effort to collect souls. There would be chaos in the streets!"

"Will you help me?" Telorithan asked impatiently. "You have a vast collection here. You've managed to obtain texts the University would not allow in its library."

The old elf beamed with pride, a smug expression settling on his wrinkled face. "It's true. My travels have afforded me some rather valuable little trinkets."

"There must be something here I can use. I need your help, Yiranor."

Yiranor couldn't help but feel sentimental at the plea of his former student. Though he was a dangerous elf to cross, he had always felt a special bond with him. Having no children of his own, he had come to look upon Telorithan as his own son. "I will do what I can," he replied. "I believe I have what you are looking for."

Telorithan smiled, knowing he had come to the right place. Yiranor was a man of wealth, and within his spire were ancient texts and artifacts that would rival even the finest museum. Though he would never admit to such things, Yiranor had dabbled in dark magic in the past. If anyone could provide the information Telorithan was seeking, it was his former master.

The old elf popped up from his seat with surprising energy. Turning to observe the shelves of his library, he lifted a finger in the air and shook it. Finally deciding on a direction, he pointed and said, "That way."

Telorithan followed closely behind as Yiranor headed for a shelf at the farthest end of the room. On a low shelf was an ornate golden chest carved with runes. Yiranor ran his hands over the lid, caressing it gently.

"This is a rare thing indeed," he said. "Inside this chest are documents written by the ancients themselves. They cover all manner of dark magics, including soul binding."

"Why didn't you show this to me immediately?" Telorithan asked, slightly offended. "You've known all along you have what I need. Why did you require me to beg?"

"Nonsense," Yiranor replied. "I only wanted you to explain a little. No harm in that, is there?"

"There could have been," Telorithan snapped. His eyes flashed red with anger, but he had no intention of harming his mentor.

A warning was fair enough, for Yiranor knew he could never defeat his former student in a duel. "You may study this here or take it with you," Yiranor offered. "I would enjoy working on this with you. I have greatly missed your presence here in my spire."

Telorithan rolled his eyes. He had no need for the old elf's emotional connection. Knowledge and power were far more important than any friendship. "If you have knowledge, then I suggest you share it."

Yiranor nodded and lifted the chest from its shelf. "Let's have a look at these scrolls, shall we?" he said as he proceeded to a long wooden table. Placing the chest on the table, he opened the lid and took out four scrolls. "I looked at these nearly a thousand years ago and haven't taken them out since. I admit I read about the practice, but I never tried to cast a binding spell. The idea was tempting, but I didn't have the desire to harm anyone by practicing on them."

"And that's why you failed to learn," Telorithan said. "I will not fail."

Chapter 5

Early the following morning, Kaiya stepped outside to bask in the warm glow of the sun. The storm had left no trace of its presence the night before, and the dark clouds had all flown away. As she made her way across the pasture, a black-and-tan herding dog came bounding toward her, his tail wagging frantically.

"Good morning, Doozle," she said, scratching the dog behind one ear. He licked her hand in reply, and the two of them continued until they reached her father and the small flock of sheep he was taking to town.

"You look much better this morning," Darvil observed.

"I feel much better," she replied. "Can I come to town with you?"

"Might as well," he replied with a shrug.

The trio set off for town, following the dirt path that led away from their farm. All the while, Doozle nudged the sheep along, taking pride in a job well done. The pace was slow and casual, the sheep having no desire to be quickly sold at market.

The mountain air still had a touch of coolness to it, despite the impending arrival of summer. Kaiya enjoyed the fresh air, which still smelled of the previous night's rain. Mountain winters could be rather cruel, and she was determined to enjoy every moment of the warm-weather season. Descending slightly through the mountains, the village awaited just ahead of them in the distance.

"I suppose I should have brought some of Mum's knitting to market," Kaiya said. "She'll be unhappy with me that I didn't."

"Too late now," Darvil replied.

Her father had never taken much interest in conversation, so Kaiya decided to walk in silence the rest of the way.

The town was already bustling with activity when they arrived. Many farmers and craftsmen had set up stalls to peddle their goods. Miners were passing by in large groups, heading for the caves where sparkling treasures patiently awaited their arrival. Soon the mountains would ring with the sound of their hammers.

As she neared the town, Kaiya's head started to feel heavy. Once again she felt the nausea in her stomach, but she did her best to shake it off. She could feel a strong magical presence but had no idea what it might be. To her knowledge, she was the only living dwarf with any magical abilities.

"You look pale, child," Darvil said, placing a hand on his daughter's arm. "Are you sick again?"

Kaiya shook her head. "I'm fine, Papa. I need only to sit a moment." She took a seat on the stone steps that led into the village. "You go on ahead," she said.

With a sigh, Darvil turned and headed into town with his sheep. Doozle whimpered and lay down on the grass next to Kaiya. She stroked his soft fur, happy to have his companionship. A gentle breeze caressed her face, and she closed her eyes as if to block out the world. Focusing only on her breathing, she felt less sick.

Suddenly, she felt as if someone were watching her, and she jumped to her feet. Looking around, she could see no one nearby. The feeling, however, did not leave her. Something was definitely aware of her presence, as she was of it. Her heart pounded in her chest as she entered the town. The feeling only became stronger, leading her to the far end of town near the mining caves. Doozle trotted along beside her, completely unaware of her concern.

As she approached one of the caves, an intense feeling of dread overcame her, forcing her to take a step back. Breathing deeply to regain her composure, she swallowed once and continued forward. Cautiously, she entered the cave, curious as to what she might find.

Inside it was completely still, and the air was cool and damp. The metallic ringing of hammers in the depths of the cave filled her ears, making it difficult to concentrate. Her nerves were beginning to take over, and she hesitated to go deeper into the cave. Drawn forward only by her curiosity, she resolved to find the source of the magic she was sensing.

The cave walls sparkled as she moved between the oil lamps affixed to the walls. Following the mining path, she inched deeper inside. The pounding in her chest grew stronger, along with the throbbing in her head. Surely she was approaching whatever magic was causing her discomfort.

"Halt there, girl!" a voice rang out from the darkness.

Startled, Kaiya stopped in her tracks. A man with a torch was approaching her, marching heavily on the stone floor.

"What are you doing here?" he demanded.

"I, I...," Kaiya stumbled. Her gray eyes flashed with magic as she searched for the correct words to say.

"I know you," the dwarf said angrily. "You're that witch girl. You're the one causing the problems with the mines. Get out of here or I'll give you a sound beating!" He swung his torch angrily at her.

Kaiya moved back, avoiding the swinging torch. Doozle barked aggressively at the miner, ready to defend his friend.

"Get that mutt out of here too!" he demanded.

"There's something inside this cave," Kaiya replied hotly. "I can sense it."

"Damn right there is," he replied. "There's a witch in here, and there's going to be trouble if she doesn't get out!"

Kaiya's eyes continued to flash as she suppressed the anger inside her. "You're an old fool," she said.

"There's something magical in here, and I'm probably the only person around here who can figure out what it is."

"It's a curse you've left on us, no doubt," the dwarf spat.

Several miners had come to witness the commotion and were standing close behind the man with the torch.

"She's the one," one of them whispered. "She put the spell on us."

Kaiya wrinkled her brow, clueless as to what they meant. "I haven't done anything," she insisted. "I came only to see what it was I felt. There is a magical being inside this cave."

"Yes, and if she doesn't get out, I'm going to bury a pickaxe in her skull!" A miner stepped forward raising his weapon high in the air.

Doozle continued to bark, but Kaiya pulled him back. "Come on," she said as she backed away from the crowd. As she turned to leave, a rock hit her on the shoulder. Soon, several of the miners were throwing rocks at her, forcing her to run from the cave.

Outside in the daylight, a few miners were about to enter the cave for work. They stared untrustingly at

Kaiya as she fled, but none of them spoke a word. Hurrying back to the market, Kaiya looked among the crowd for her father. Spotting him near the smithy, she slowed her pace and approached him.

"Papa," she said. "There's magic in one of the mining caves. I couldn't tell what it was before the miners chased me out. I think it might be dangerous."

Darvil and Ortin, the blacksmith, exchanged glances.

"They accused me of being a witch and said I'd cursed them," she continued.

"There are rumors of sickness in the mines," Ortin said. "They must think you're the cause." Ortin's dark eyes looked sympathetically at Kaiya.

"That's the stupidest thing I've ever heard," Darvil replied. "She'd never harm a soul!"

"People have always been suspicious of her," Ortin remarked. "She's different, and they're ignorant."

"My magic isn't used for curses," Kaiya said. "I have never studied such a thing. Why would they think I want to hurt them?"

"Because they don't know any better," Darvil said. "We've kept you shut away too much, I suppose. We should have brought you to town more so people could see that you weren't any different from them."

"I stayed away because they were mean to me, Papa. You didn't have anything to do with it. It was my choice."

"They don't seem to have trouble with the magic runes that Trin carves," Ortin said. "But that's not the same as what you can do." He stroked his black beard before continuing. "You can conjure magic from the air. No dwarf in my lifetime has done such a thing. They don't know what to think of you."

"They can think whatever they like, but that's no excuse to be ugly. They threw stones at me." Her voice was full of contempt.

"They trust magic that comes from a hammer and chisel," Darvil said. "They don't trust what they can't understand. I don't understand it myself, but I know you wouldn't hurt anyone."

"There she is!" The dwarf she had first met in the cave had followed her back to town. "She's the one who caused the illness, and I caught her in the cave making sure the curse stuck!"

"That's a lie!" she shouted back.

Some of the townsfolk looked up from their work, straining to hear what the yelling was about. A few of them felt brave enough to approach. Darvil stepped between his daughter and the angry miner.

"Listen here," he stated. "If you raise one hand to my daughter again, you'll have me to deal with."

"Take that witch of yours and get out of here, farmer," the dwarf replied. "Get out of here before there's trouble."

"You're standing in my smithy," Ortin broke in. "You can get out of *here* before there's trouble." Ortin gripped a large hammer tightly in his hand and lifted it so the miner could see he was serious.

"You better lift that curse, witch," he said, pointing at Kaiya. With those words, he turned and headed back to the caves.

"I don't need you to fight my battles, but thank you," Kaiya said.

"You start using your magic against them and there will be real trouble," her father warned. "It's best to let us deal with it." He nodded his thanks to Ortin and took his daughter by the arm. "Let's get back home," he said.

Reluctantly, Kaiya joined him on the road home and maintained her silence. She was determined to find the source of the magic and learn whether it had anything to do with the illness Ortin had mentioned. Worry lay heavily on her mind as she walked, while Doozle trotted alongside without a care in the world.

Chapter 6

Stepping up onto the riverbank, River glanced around at the gathered crowd. Ryllak motioned for his son to follow him as he walked away from the commotion.

"What did the Spirit tell you?" he asked.

"Only that there is a sickness among the dwarves in the mountains. There is evil there."

Ryllak looked at the ground and back at his son. "Did the Spirit say what this sickness is? Are our people in danger?"

"He did not say," River replied, shaking his head.

Pushing his way through the crowd, Galen came to River's side. "Looks like there's a bit of excitement here today," he said with a smirk.

Ryllak gave him a chiding look, displeased with the young elf's cheerful disposition. "This isn't something to be made light of," he said. "There is trouble in the mountains, and trouble could always make its way here."

"My apologies," Galen replied, bowing his head slightly and biting his lip.

River sighed, glancing between his father and Galen. "What will they do with the body?"

"It will be taken to Myla at the House of Medicine. She will make arrangements for it." Ryllak glanced back over his shoulder at the dwarf. The elves were lifting him onto a stretcher for transport.

"Couldn't we take him back to his family?" River asked.

"That would prove a difficult task," Ryllak replied. "It's a long journey into the mountains. I think it's best we deal with his remains here."

"We should at least inform his kinsmen, don't you think?" Galen asked. "There has to be some way to send a message. Maybe River can do it." He slapped River on the arm jokingly in an effort to lighten the mood. Serious situations made him uncomfortable, and he was usually too quick to make a joke. This time, he tried to be on his best behavior.

"Maybe," River replied. "I'm not sure."

"Let's go to the House of Medicine. Maybe Myla will let us watch her examine him." Galen seemed eager to get away from Ryllak.

"Try not to get in her way," Ryllak suggested as he turned to leave.

The pair followed the elves who were carrying the dwarf's body through the village. The crowd had finally dispersed, and the elves were busying themselves with their duties beneath the silver trees of the Vale. The sun shone brightly, and the birds sang with joy despite the events of the morning. It seemed as if nothing out of the ordinary had occurred.

"She doesn't like me," River said.

"Who, Myla?" Galen asked.

"Yes," he replied. "She's always scowling at me, no matter how hard I try to be polite to her. I can't recall doing anything to offend her, but she hates me just the same."

"She doesn't know you is all," Galen said, trying to ease his friend's mind.

As they arrived at the wide silver tree, they paused for a moment to allow the elves carrying the body to enter. Slowly they marched through the arched doorways of the House of Medicine and laid the lifeless dwarf onto a cot. Galen and River stepped inside quietly.

"What is this?" Myla asked, rising from her desk. Her blond hair was pulled tightly back into a ponytail, giving her slender face an even thinner appearance.

"We bring you the body of a dwarf who fell to his death from the mountains," one of the elves said.

"I want nothing to do with dwarves," she replied coldly. "Take it elsewhere."

River bravely spoke up, knowing that Myla was not one to take kindly to an argument. "Mistress," he began, "this dwarf was suffering from an illness before he fell. Your medical knowledge is needed to determine if it is a threat to us."

She narrowed her eyes, staring at River. "The Westerling Elves do not suffer natural disease. Being some sort of hybrid elf, I expect you did not know that."

"I have lived in the Vale for two hundred years, Mistress," River replied, trying not to sound disrespectful. "I know we are not susceptible to most disease, but this may be brought on by magic."

"I want nothing to do with it," she declared haughtily. "One of my assistants may look at it if any of them are willing." She turned her back to River and resumed working at her desk.

Stepping outside into the sunlight, Galen said, "That went well."

River stared at him, annoyed by the comment. "I shouldn't have gone in. I should have let the others convey the message."

"River, it's not you she hates. It's your father."

Taken aback, River said, "My father? Why would she hate him?"

Laughing at first, Galen asked, "Don't you remember that time you fell out of the giant almond tree at the far edge of the Vale?"

"Yes." River had no idea what an event from so long ago had to do with anything.

"You landed with a splash and a thud, and I nearly died laughing." He chuckled and continued, "When you didn't get up right away, I got worried. I ran back to the village to get Myla, but as soon as she knelt down to check your pulse, Ryllak walked over and scooped you up. He told her not to worry as he carried you back to the river and tossed you in. She hasn't liked either of you since that day."

"He didn't toss me. He sat me at the edge," River replied.

"Well, he—wait," Galen said. "You were unconscious. How do you know what he did?"

"I wasn't completely unconscious," he said with a shrug. "I knew what was going on around me, but I couldn't seem to wake up—until he put me in the water, of course. Anyway, that seems a silly reason for her to dislike either of us. We didn't need her help, that's all."

"Yes, and she thinks everyone should always need her advice." Galen grinned at River, feeling proud of his explanation.

River shook his head and laughed despite himself. "You have a unique perspective on things, Galen."

Galen beamed proudly. "I know it. If you weren't always trying to be all mystical and elementalish you'd see things as clearly as I do."

"I'll keep that in mind," River replied. "What do we do now?"

"I think I know someone who will examine the dwarf for us," Galen said. "Follow me."

Chapter 7

Deep in the forests of the Vale, Lenora sat patiently awaiting the arrival of her dryad sisters. Though she was an elf, she had spent the past several years studying under the guidance of the dryads. Her talent for healing arts was well nurtured here among the forests, and she enjoyed learning as much as she could.

The dryads had taught her about dozens of different plants and their medicinal properties. Through their knowledge of earth magic, they had also taught her new spells that could be used to heal the sick. The trees themselves were not immune to disease, and Lenora was still learning how best to go about healing them. Though her kind were not susceptible to most diseases, it was a skill worth learning and remembering. Times were uncertain, and it was best to remain prepared.

A silvery-skinned dryad made her way to Lenora, her leafy hair fluttering on the breeze as she walked. The sunlight filtered down through the trees, giving her skin a shimmery appearance. Though her body seemed covered in rough bark, her skin was quite soft.

"Well met, Sister," the silver dryad said.

"Good morning," Lenora replied.

The two sat side by side on a fallen log. Lenora was eager to show her dryad sister a salve she had been working on, hoping she had gotten the ingredients correct this time. She handed the ceramic bowl filled with yellow-green paste to the dryad.

"It's the right color this time," she said approvingly. Holding up the bowl to her nose, she breathed deeply, inhaling the strong odor of the salve. "I think you've got it right this time. Let's test it."

Rising from the log, Lenora followed the dryad to a berry bush whose leaves had been covered in dark blotches. The plant looked wilted and sorrowful, and it was plainly suffering from disease.

Handing the dish to Lenora, the dryad said, "Apply a small amount to the leaves, and place the rest at its base."

Lenora obeyed, gently rubbing the salve into each leaf of the ailing plant. There were many leaves, and the task required a great amount of delicacy to avoid further damaging them. Methodically she tended each leaf, all the while willing her mind to focus healing energy. Placing her hands at the plant's base, her eyes began to sparkle. A white glow spread from her hands and down into the earth, making its way deep into the soil. As the plant's roots started to heal, the wilted leaves once again regained their strength.

"The spots will take time to heal, but you have done well," the dryad said.

Lenora smiled sweetly and brushed a hand over the leaves. "Earth magic is truly a wonder," she said, standing.

"Earth magic has no room for selfishness or corruption," the dryad replied. "What you have learned will help you as a healer of all living things."

"I believe you are right," Lenora agreed. "I have learned many things here among your kind. I was not born with a talent for earth magic, and I had no idea I would ever learn any of it. You've truly opened my eyes to new possibilities."

"There is much more you will learn in time, Lenora," the dryad stated assuredly. "There is much still ahead of you, and there are other magical creatures willing to teach you."

Lenora was intrigued by those words. From a young age, she knew she wanted to be a healer like her mother. Her mother, however, focused only on potions and basic spells. Lenora yearned to learn from other schools of magic and to incorporate those skills into the healing arts. Because they were not susceptible to disease and had almost no contact with the outside world, the Westerling Elves had forgotten many of the skills necessary to heal the sick and injured. Lenora was determined to learn what had been lost.

At the sound of approaching footsteps, both Lenora and the dryad halted their conversation. Amid the deep-green foliage of the forest, they saw the outline of a dark-haired elf.

"Hello there," Galen said as he pushed his way past a low limb.

River emerged behind him, his eyes falling past the dryad and onto Lenora. His heart fluttered for a second as he looked upon her. She wore a simple apricot dress, which was easily outshone by her bright-gold tresses. The sight of her slender, shapely form silhouetted against the sunlight nearly took his breath away. Her pale eyes returned his gaze, and she smiled politely.

Galen glanced over his shoulder, making sure River was still there. Looking back to Lenora, he said, "We've come looking for you, Lenora."

With surprise, River looked at Galen, wondering how he knew this woman. Theirs was the only remaining village of Westerling Elves, and he could not recall ever meeting this lovely creature before. He did not believe it possible that he hadn't noticed her earlier.

"What do you need of me?" Lenora asked.

"You're a skilled healer, and there is some trouble in the village."

"Surely my mother can deal with it," Lenora replied, a little confused.

"Mother?" River asked, stunned. "You're Myla's daughter?" His heart dropped at the prospect.

"I am," she replied. "I've been away studying for some time, so it's no surprise you don't remember me."

River felt ashamed to have met Lenora previously and not remember her now. She was captivating, and he yearned to know her better. Finding no words, he remained silent.

61

"Your mother wants nothing to do with the matter," Galen said.

"There is an illness affecting the dwarves in the mountains," River explained. "One of them fell into the river and drowned. I believe the illness might have a magical origin, and it might have something to do with water."

Galen glanced at him, wrinkling his brow. Apparently River knew a bit more than he was sharing with his cousin.

"It sounds interesting," Lenora admitted.

"Will you come with us?" Galen asked.

Lenora turned to the dryad who nodded her approval.

"I will," she replied. "I am due to return for my Coming of Age Ceremony anyway."

River held his breath as she came nearer, unable to take his eyes off her. She blushed a little, noticing his gaze. Galen was not unaware of his friend's actions either. He shook his head and suppressed a laugh.

"So," River began awkwardly, "you're coming of age this year?"

"Last year, actually," Lenora replied with a laugh. "I've been too busy studying to bother with it."

"Fantastic," Galen broke in. "Another bookworm among us." He elbowed River playfully.

The trio marched quietly through the woods, the soft grass making little noise beneath their feet. River struggled in his mind to find some words to speak to Lenora but feared he might trip over his own tongue.

Chapter 8

After spending the past several days intensely studying the ancient scrolls, Telorithan and Yiranor were ready to attempt the forbidden magic. They had discussed the technique repeatedly as they pored over the texts, eagerly drinking in their forgotten lessons. The scrolls contained more information than Telorithan could have hoped for. Everything he needed had been locked away inside his former master's library.

"We'll be needing a test subject," Telorithan declared. "The question is, who can we use?"

Yiranor swallowed and took a deep breath. The idea of soul binding had always fascinated him, but he was hesitant to test it on a live subject. "Perhaps a rodent," he suggested.

Telorithan laughed, tossing his head back. "No, that won't do. It must be an elf."

A quiet knock came from the door before a young elf woman entered carrying a bottle of wine and two silver goblets on a tray. Yiranor motioned her to come in.

"Leave it on the table," he ordered her.

"Yes, Master," she replied. Hesitating at the door, she turned and asked, "Will you be coming down for dinner or shall I bring it up?"

Yiranor glanced at Telorithan, who was ignoring the woman. "I'll send for you when we're ready to dine," he replied. The young elf gave a polite curtsy and closed the door behind her as she left.

Telorithan eyed the closed door, a contemplative expression on his face. "There is someone we could use. Someone no one would miss."

"Not the maid," Yiranor protested. "She's a sweet girl and always does as she's told." His heart raced, fearing he might have to stand up to his former student. He wasn't sure he would have the strength, and in a fight, Telorithan was sure to win.

"Not her," Telorithan said. "You said you caught a thief prowling outside your home weeks ago. He still resides in your dungeons, does he not?"

With relief, Yiranor replied, "Yes, he does." Though the elf was a criminal, Yiranor was hesitant to use him as a test subject for dark magic.

"And he deserves to be punished," Telorithan said, attempting to persuade the old elf. "I can't think of a better person to use." He rose from his seat and grabbed the wine bottle on the wooden table nearby. Filling both glasses, he handed one to Yiranor, who slowly pressed it to his lips. Telorithan stopped for a moment to admire his reflection in the silver goblet. His stunning blue eyes sparkled with delight at the sight of himself.

After a moment's contemplation, Yiranor nodded. "It seems almost too harsh a punishment," he declared. "The scrolls say that the soul lives on in torment once bound."

"Then it's a perfect punishment," Telorithan replied, setting his goblet down hard. "Let's get started."

Hesitating for less than a second, Yiranor led his former student down the winding staircase to the lowest level of his tower. A thick iron gate barred the way into the cellar, where many of the master sorcerer's experiments had taken place. It was true he had practiced magic on elves in the past, but they had been his apprentices and were willing to undergo experimentation. This was different. He was about to engage in a forbidden act, torturing a living elf in the process.

With a wave of his hand, Telorithan unlocked the gate. The spell was simple enough to cast, and he did not have the patience to await his former master's final attempt at stalling. Swinging open the door, the two entered the gray-stone underbelly of the tower. It was surprisingly bright due to the excess of torches lining the walls. Yiranor was of advanced age and required the extra light to look upon his work.

Chained to a far wall was a dark-haired elf with large purple bruises all over his body. He made no movement at the sound of the two men approaching.

"My apprentices have been using him to train various spells," Yiranor admitted.

Telorithan nodded approvingly. He moved in close to the prisoner, looking him up and down. The thief shifted uneasily in his chains, sensing the danger he was about to face. Telorithan met his gaze, and a wicked smile spread across his lips.

"This should be fun," he said.

The chained elf began to breathe heavier, his chest visibly rising and falling. Telorithan was amused by the elf's fear, but Yiranor was having second thoughts.

"Perhaps we should—" he started to say.

Throwing up a hand to silence the old elf, Telorithan loudly commanded him to hold his tongue. "I will take care of this. You can go and hide if you need to." He had lost all patience with his former master. No one would deprive him of this opportunity to practice.

"Release me and fight fairly, at least," the thief stated boldly. "Or are you frightened of me?"

His words angered Telorithan, and he lifted both hands, sending flames through the shackles that held the thief to the wall. As the metal changed from cool gray to red, the elf screamed in agony. The metal soon liquefied and dripped to the floor, forming two small silver puddles. The thief sank to his knees, cradling each wrist in turn. His skin was blistered and darkened where the shackles had been.

"You may resist if you can," Telorithan said with a huff. From the pocket of his robe, he pulled a pale-purple gemstone that was nearly the size of a walnut. Holding it tightly in his left hand, he extended his right palm forward toward the thief. A beam of purple light emitted from his hand and quickly surrounded the kneeling elf. Yiranor could not contain a gasp as he stepped backward away from the magic.

A cry of agony pierced the air as the thief was lifted from his feet. Excitement rose in Telorithan's eyes as he concentrated on his target. His left hand trembled slightly as the gem called for the essence it desired to contain. Opening his left hand to allow the magic to pass, the beam dissipated from his right hand while the glow released its hold on the thief. The elf crumpled lifelessly to the ground, leaving only a small circular light where he had once knelt. The light drifted slowly toward the gem in Telorithan's hand and flashed brightly as it entered its prison. The spell had been successful.

Telorithan held up the gem to examine it. His eyes gleamed as he beheld the swirling mist of light inside the stone. The thief's essence had been contained, and his power now rested fully under Telorithan's control.

"Remarkable," Yiranor whispered as he stepped forward once more. "You've done it."

"Of course I have," Telorithan replied haughtily, sticking the gem back into his pocket. "Why would you ever doubt me?"

"I wouldn't dream of it," Yiranor replied apologetically. "That thief had been down here for weeks, though. You might find a stronger enemy more difficult to contain."

Telorithan wrinkled his brow and stared at him. "You think I can't handle a real sorcerer?"

Concerned for his own safety, Yiranor quickly replied, "No, I only mean you may need more practice. This was only your first attempt on an elf."

"You could be right," Telorithan admitted. "Are you volunteering yourself?" He laughed, knowing that his former master feared him.

Yiranor could not hide the embarrassment on his face. "I will do what I can to help you," he said. "You know I will."

"Good," Telorithan replied. "I may have need of you again. For now, I'll be going. There is much I still need to prepare."

Yiranor nodded and watched as his former pupil headed back up the stairs of his tower. *The Sunswept Isles will never be safe with him around. His heart is dark, and this new skill will only make him worse.* For a brief moment, Yiranor regretted his involvement in aiding Telorithan to learn this dark magic. He would be partially responsible for any deaths that resulted. Still, he could not help but feel pride in the young elf he had once nurtured. His ambition had already taken him far, and now with the ability to extract the life essence from his opponents, Telorithan would be unstoppable. His dream of trapping the soul of a god might not prove so far out of his reach.

Chapter 9

Darkness settled over the mountains. The stars hid themselves behind the clouds, but the moon's glow fought its way through the thickness, providing a dim, hazy light. The wind gently rustled the leaves on the trees, and the creatures of the night sang softly to the sky.

Kaiya lay awake in her bed, unable to put her mind at ease. Earlier in the evening, her father had expressly forbidden her to go anywhere near town, thanks to the hostility the pair had encountered. No matter her age, he would always think of her as a child who needed his protection. She was the youngest of his children and had no husband, which gave her father the excuse he needed to carry on in the role of her protector.

She understood her father's need to protect her, but it wasn't necessary. Kaiya was not an average dwarf girl who was expected only to have children and run a home. Her magical powers were strong, and she had spent her life honing her talents. Without the distraction of friends and their silly childhood games, Kaiya was able to spend her days practicing magic and teaching herself to harness the wind. She was not helpless. She was a strong woman who could look after herself.

As quietly as she could manage, Kaiya rose from her bed and headed for the front door. Her urge to discover the presence in the caves was far stronger than her need to listen to her father's warnings. She did not fear the miners. Their weapons were nothing compared to her powers. The magical being within the cave, however, was something unknown. She could not decide whether it was malevolent, and she wanted to know if it was the source of the illness that had been spreading among the miners.

As she tiptoed to the door in the darkness, she reached out with her hand to avoid tripping on any unseen obstacles in her path. To her surprise, her cloak had been hung on the doorknob, and a wooden torch was propped against the door as well. *Mum,* she thought. Somehow her mother knew she would be going out tonight, even before Kaiya herself had made up her mind to do so.

Stepping out into the night, she quietly closed the door behind her. Her magic could provide her with excellent night vision, but she decided to light the torch instead. She did not want to waste any magical energy that she might need later inside the cave. Creeping across the yard, she hoped Doozle would not bark and wake her parents before she could reach the dirt road that would lead her to town.

The nighttime air in the mountains was cool despite it being early summer. She pulled her cloak a bit closer to her skin, but the chill she felt had more to do with her nerves than the weather. She could sense the magic emitting from deep inside the cave and felt compelled to investigate.

Her pace quickened as her eyes adjusted to the dark. The torch in her hand provided enough light to save her from tripping over the rocks along the path. Images of monsters from childhood tales flashed in her mind as she tried to prepare herself for what might await her in the cave. Never in her life had she encountered true evil. Ignorance and prejudice had presented themselves, but not evil. The monsters were not real, but something real was in the caves, and she feared it might be the true cause of the illness.

Reaching the edge of town, she doused the flame on her torch to avoid being noticed. Being after midnight, the town was deserted, and all the dwarves were safely tucked away in their homes. If this night proved dangerous for Kaiya, there was little chance of assistance from her kinsmen.

A single night watchman stood guard outside the cave. More security was not necessary, since most dwarves did not easily turn to a life of crime. Severe punishments, including loss of limb, had been used in the past, and that had deterred most criminal behavior for centuries. The watchman was responsible mainly for keeping out vandals and teenage lovers looking for a bit of privacy.

The silver-bearded dwarf stood at the ready with no sign of drowsiness apparent in his posture. Taking great care to stay hidden, Kaiya slowly lifted a hand and closed her eyes. A gentle gust of wind passed by the guard, gaining momentum as it traveled. In the nearby mining camp, a cart began to roll and quickly crashed into a rickety wooden table, overturning both in the process. A loud clang was followed by a crash as used dishes toppled from the table to the ground.

A little too much, she thought, promising to hold back a bit next time.

The guard readied a large hammer in his hand and trudged off to investigate the disturbance. Kaiya made a dash for the cave with only the moonlight to guide her path. Safely inside the cave, the sound of dripping water filled her ears. Proceeding deeper within, the light became dimmer and dimmer, until she was forced to use magic to see. Her eyes sparkled with silver as she willed herself to see in the pitch-black surroundings.

The walls shimmered and reflected the light from her eyes. An overwhelming sense of foreboding came over her, and she hesitated in her steps. Taking a deep breath, she knew she would have to continue to find the source of the magic. Her heart pounded in her ears, but her feet kept moving forward.

She paused again deep within the cave where a rock formation resembling a large basin glistened white among the gray interior. From the ceiling, a second white formation descended, providing a rain shower into the tub below. The water rushed forth with great strength, and the sound echoed loudly from the walls. Directly behind the tub, a clear pool lay motionless. As she peered into the pool, she saw the reflection of the ceiling, which made the water appear to delve deep into eternity. She glimpsed her own face among the water and smiled slightly, amused at the sight of her eyes as they sparkled with magic.

A white light started to form at the edge of the pool, circling inward and becoming ever brighter. The apparition of an elf maiden in a white dress appeared, hovering above the center of the pool. Kaiya lifted her arm to shield her eyes from the sudden light.

"Leave me to my sorrow and malice!" a loud voice boomed.

Kaiya flinched at the sound of the voice. Clearly this being was upset by her presence. "Who are you?" she asked.

"That is not your concern," she replied. "Be gone from this place!"

Kaiya swallowed hard and looked into the elf's eyes. "I won't leave until I know what you are," she replied defiantly.

A beam of white light shot forth, but Kaiya reacted in time. Holding a hand up, she deflected the beam, which bounced between the cave's walls before fading away.

"I am a being of magic as well," she declared. "I will not harm you, and you should not be trying to harm me. Tell me how I can help you." Kaiya's words were sincere. If she could release this creature from her sorrow, she would do whatever was necessary.

"Be gone!" the elf repeated.

"Are you the one making the miners ill?" Kaiya asked, ignoring the order to leave. Another bolt of light flew toward her, but she was ready for it. With both hands, she repelled the attack, sending the light back to the apparition. The elf took on a stronger glow but was unharmed.

"You must leave, child," the elf said in a melancholy voice. "You do not belong here."

Before she could protest, the water from the pool began to rise, forcing Kaiya to higher ground. The more she moved, the more the water rose. Within seconds, the cave had filled with water to the height of her shoulders. Not knowing what else to do, Kaiya turned and swam as best she could away from the elf maiden.

Once the apparition believed Kaiya was leaving, the water receded. To her dismay, the dwarf girl returned as soon as the water level was low enough for her to stand. She strode boldly forward to face the elf once more.

"You haven't answered my question," Kaiya stated.

"I can see you learn slowly," the elf replied. "It seems I must teach you not to meddle with magic you couldn't possibly understand."

Kaiya stood firm, bracing herself for another attack.

Chapter 10

River walked between Galen and Lenora as the three of them headed back to their village. The forest buzzed with activity all around them, providing plenty of distractions from the silence. Occasionally, River glanced at Lenora as if to say something but turned his head away again without speaking. Lenora smiled to herself as she walked, sensing River's insecurity.

"How long have you studied with the dryads?" he finally managed to ask.

Lenora replied, "About two years now. They've taught me many things."

River could not think of a suitable follow-up question to continue the conversation. The light bouncing off Lenora's golden locks filled his vision, and he failed to find his words.

"Do they do anything but plant trees?" Galen asked, filling the silence.

"They do many things within the forest," Lenora replied. "They understand every bird's song, and they know each blade of grass. They could teach me such things if I had the ability to learn them. As elves, we are limited in what we are able to understand of this world. The dryads have a powerful connection to the earth that we lack." She paused in her walking to look at River. "You may be less limited, or more so. I'm not sure which."

"How do you mean?" River asked.

"Well, you aren't just an elf, are you?" She smiled and cocked her head slightly to the side. River felt his ears turning red and hoped she did not notice. Galen glanced at River, giving a nod of approval.

Finally, they arrived in the village and made their way to the House of Medicine.

"I have to warn you that your mother might not be happy I've involved you in this," River admitted.

"She has her own way of doing things, and I have mine," Lenora said. "If she refused to do the work, then I must do it instead." Opening the door, she added, "Let's see if we can't figure out what happened to your dwarf."

Myla sat inside at her desk. At the sight of her daughter, she rose to her feet. "Lenora?" she asked, surprised. "What brings you here?"

"My friends have requested my assistance. It seems there is trouble among the dwarves."

"Don't concern yourself with that," she replied coldly. "There are others who can tend to it."

"Nevertheless, I'm here, and I would be happy to look into it." To her mother's dismay, she proceeded to the dwarf's lifeless body, which had been encased in magic to preserve it for the time being.

She peeled away the magical layers to examine the dwarf. As she touched him, her hands emitted a white glow. "You were right about it being a magical illness," she said, looking up at River. "He was cursed."

"The two of you should leave now," Myla broke in. "I need to speak with my daughter."

"Thank you for your help, Lenora," River said before turning to leave.

Galen flashed a devilish grin at Myla before walking out the door. Myla narrowed her eyes in response and glared at the two as they walked away.

"What are you doing with them?" Myla asked.

Lenora sat casually next to the body of the dwarf. "They came to find me. They said there was trouble."

She shrugged and turned her attention back to the dwarf.

"That elf may be dangerous," Myla continued. "We don't know what he is."

"Who? River?" Lenora replied with a dismissing wave of her hand. "He's harmless."

"That thing in the water killed his mother, and it inhabits him. He's only just come of age, and we don't know what he's capable of."

"I can take care of myself, Mother."

Myla took a step closer to the dwarf's body and inspected it. "I don't want you involved in this matter either," she declared. "I will handle it."

"Too late," Lenora replied playfully. "I'm already involved."

"You have a Coming of Age Ceremony to worry about. Set your mind to that, and I will deal with this."

Lenora shook her head but appeared to comply with her mother's wish as she made her way to the exit. Still trying to work out the cause of the dwarf's demise, she stepped out into the sunlight. River and Galen stood on the opposite side of the door, and she nearly bumped into them.

"Hello again," she said with a laugh.

"I take it your mother isn't happy we involved you in this," Galen said.

"No, she isn't."

"Forgive me if I've caused you trouble," River said earnestly. He gazed into her pale eyes as he spoke and nearly forgot what he was talking about.

"It's no trouble," she replied. "Shall we sit and talk a while?"

"Certainly," River answered, his heart fluttering in his chest. He glanced at Galen, who was grinning from ear to ear.

Not wanting to intrude, Galen said, "I can't. I have to...," he thought for a second, "go pluck a hair."

River's mouth dropped open slightly, and he buried his face in his hand. His embarrassment was genuine, but Galen laughed and slapped him on the shoulder.

Lenora burst out laughing. "Let us know if you need any help with that."

"Will do," Galen said. He waved cheerfully at the pair before leaving them to each other's company.

River and Lenora took a seat on a silver bench under the shade of a large tree.

"So," Lenora began, "what brought you out into the woods to find me?"

"Galen," River replied. "He said you could help us figure out what was going on." He fidgeted nervously with his hands as he spoke.

Smiling, Lenora said, "My mother isn't a fan of dwarves. Or of anyone, for that matter. I'm glad you came to find me."

River stopped fidgeting and smiled at her, hoping her last comment meant she was happy to meet him. "You said the dwarf was cursed," he said, attempting to prolong the conversation.

"Yes," she replied. "It was definitely some dark magic that caused his death. He had been quite ill, but the sickness progressed much faster than anything of natural causes would do."

"The Spirit of the river told me there was evil in the mountains."

Curiously, Lenora asked, "What do you and the Spirit usually talk about? I hear you speak with it every day."

"Some days it tells me nothing. Other days it tells me too much." He shook his head. "Sometimes I don't understand what it's telling me."

"You've learned stronger magic from it, right?" Lenora asked, leaning closer to River.

"Yes, it has taught me quite a bit. I still need practice, though. It isn't quite the same as the magic we learned in school."

Lenora smiled warmly and said, "I imagine it's quite different. The dryads are teaching me new magic as well."

As the conversation tapered off, the two young elves sat in silence. It was nearing sunset before they finally decided it was time to part ways.

"I should probably be going," Lenora said. "I have one more question for you. Is the Spirit of the river dangerous?"

"No, I don't believe it is," he replied, unsure why she was asking.

"Are you dangerous?"

River stared at her a moment before answering. "No, of course not." He didn't understand why she would ask such a thing. He had never done anything that would make the other elves afraid of him, and there was nothing he could do to change the circumstance of his birth.

"I didn't think so," she replied, her eyes sparkling. Leaning in, she kissed him softly on his cheek. "I'll see you tomorrow," she said.

River watched as she walked away. His head felt as if it were about to burst, and he had to remind himself to breathe. Lenora was the most beautiful creature he had ever seen, and he knew he was in love with her. Whether she felt the same way, he could not be sure. For now, having her friendship would have to be enough.

Chapter 11

Kaiya stood her ground, staring straight at the apparition. Summoning her courage, she said, "Tell me why you are harming the miners. What have they done to you?"

The ground shook as the apparition lifted her arms into the air.

"Please!" Kaiya screamed. "Tell me how I can make things right!"

The elf's translucent body glowed brighter, and Kaiya suddenly felt it difficult to breathe. A crushing sensation spread throughout her chest, and her throat felt as if it were being gripped by a strong hand.

"Be gone!" the booming voice of the apparition shouted again.

In fear for her life, Kaiya turned to flee. Choking and gasping for air, she ran as fast as she could through the darkness and out of the cave.

The guard, who had returned to his post, was surprised to see someone running from the cave. "Halt there!" he shouted.

Kaiya had no intention of stopping and continued to run. The guard pursued for a few moments but lost her to the black of night. The farther she ran from the cave, the easier it was to breathe. She paused for a moment behind a boulder to catch her breath. Her entire body shook with fear, and she hated herself for losing courage.

I'm no closer to an answer, she thought. The magic within the cave was the strongest she had ever encountered. It was obvious she couldn't combat it, and she feared for the lives of the miners. The apparition was a creature of evil—full of anger and hate. Never before had Kaiya encountered such malice.

Slowly she followed the rocky dirt path that would lead her home. Dawn was breaking as she arrived at the edge of her farm. Burying her face in her hands, she sat on the grass and wept. There was no way to know if she had made things worse by angering the spirit in the cave. More dwarves could be harmed by her actions, even though she had gone with only the intention to do good.

As she sat in silence, a gust of wind came along to dry the tears from her face. *Where were you when I needed you?* In the caves, she had not felt the presence of the wind. Her magic had been far too weak without it. Kaiya drew in a deep breath and let it out slowly. Closing her eyes, she held her face to the breeze. She could not help but smile as it caressed her tear-stained cheeks. *I'll just have to try again,* she thought. To the wind, she said, "Don't abandon me this time."

The door to the farmhouse creaked as Darvil stepped out to perform his morning chores. His thick red beard danced around him on the strong breeze. Kaiya rose in time to see Doozle running from the barn, his tongue lolling out in greeting. She waved to her father and patted the herding dog on his head.

"What's got you up so early?" Darvil asked.

"I couldn't sleep," she replied, bending down to give Doozle a good rub on his shoulder. "Are you heading to town today?"

"Sure am," he replied. "I'm not sure things have cooled down enough for you to come along," he admitted.

"I don't want to come," she responded. "I'm curious to hear if there's any news."

"I'll bring back what I can," he promised.

Kaiya headed into the house to collect her mother's knitting. Dishes clanged in the kitchen, suggesting Kassie was already up as well. Placing the finished scarves and hats into a canvas bag, Kaiya placed it outside the door for her father to take into town. Kassie spent most of her day dying wool and knitting items for the townsfolk, and her work brought in a good amount of extra money. Their family was by no means wealthy, but at least there was money for items they couldn't craft themselves.

A steaming bowl of porridge awaited Kaiya on the kitchen table. She took a seat and added some honey to her bowl before taking a bite.

"Careful, it's hot," Kassie warned without turning around.

Kaiya shook her head, resigning herself to the fact that her mother would always think of her as a child. Being the baby of the family did have its advantages, but sometimes it was nice to be treated as an adult.

"What were you up to last night?" Kassie asked.

"What makes you think I was up to something?" she replied through a mouthful of porridge.

"Are we answering questions with questions today?" Her mother gave her a quizzical look and took a seat across from her. "I know you were out, and I'm worried about you. Going to town isn't safe."

Kaiya sighed. "You always seem to know what I'm going to do before I do it. Yes, I went to town to investigate the magic I felt in the cave."

"And?"

"And I didn't find much. There is a presence there, and she isn't happy. She wants to harm the miners, but I don't know why. All I know is she's far more powerful than me. I don't know why she's making people ill, and I don't know how to stop her." Kaiya turned her attention back to her breakfast to hide her frustration.

"You need guidance is all," her mother said, attempting to comfort her.

"There isn't anyone to guide me," she replied, shaking her head. "There never has been."

"There are schools among the elves of the islands." Kassie knew Kaiya was already aware of such places, but it couldn't hurt to remind her.

"They aren't going to accept me, Mum," Kaiya replied. "They barely accept elves into those schools. I will have to figure this out on my own."

Kassie stood and kissed her daughter on the head before leaving Kaiya to eat in peace. As the silence crept into her ears, Kaiya once again turned her thoughts to the being in the cave. There had to be a way to stop her before more dwarves fell ill—or worse. A hard road lay before her, but she would not give in to despair. She would find a way to save her kinsmen, no matter how difficult it seemed. If her magic wasn't yet strong enough, she would have to find a way to supplement it.

Chapter 12

Sirra stood patiently in the waiting area of Telorithan's tower. The raven-haired enchantress wore a form-fitting black dress that emphasized her ample curves. She sighed, wondering how long Telorithan would keep her waiting today. He always kept her waiting as if she were not an important guest to meet. In reality, she was probably his only friend. Despite his many flaws, Sirra cared more for him than any other man.

With only servants available for conversation, Sirra preferred to wait in solitude. Even though he had achieved the rank of Master nearly two centuries ago, Telorithan had never taken on any apprentices. He simply did not have the patience for them, and he had no intention of giving away his arcane secrets to mere students. Sirra herself had barely been let in on his experiments, and that had taken a lot of work on her part. Convincing him to trust her had taken many years.

Finally giving in to her fatigue, she took a seat near the window. The street below provided little in the way of distraction since Telorithan's tower was built far from the cities, giving him the silence he demanded for his work. The tower's interior was sparse on decoration. There were scores of books and scrolls but barely enough furnishings to fill the inhabited rooms. Lacking any apprentices, the majority of the tower's bedrooms remained empty and unused.

Sirra had often commented that a woman's touch was badly needed in his home. She was not so subtle about her willingness to become his partner and had offered to move in on several occasions. Telorithan was not the sort of elf who needed a companion around, and he had refused her request each time. Sirra had her own work to tend to, so she eventually resigned herself to living apart from him. At the very least, she knew there was no one else in his bed at night, and that gave her some comfort.

After making her wait more than an hour, Telorithan finally made his way down the twisted staircase to meet his guest. As he entered the sitting room, Sirra quickly stood, turning her body slightly to the side to emphasize her figure. Her ankle-length gown was split up both sides, giving him a thorough view of her thighs. He rolled his eyes, knowing exactly why she had come to visit him.

"Telorithan, love," she said, moving forward to take his hand. "It seems forever since we last spoke."

"I've had more important matters to occupy my time," he said coldly, drawing his hand away. He took a seat near the fireplace and leaned his head on his hand as if bored. "I see you haven't come for scholarly purposes." He raised his eyebrows and looked her up and down once more.

"Indeed not," she admitted, a flirtatious smile spreading across her ruby lips.

"I'm busy, Sirra. I don't have time for social calls."

"Then perhaps I can assist you in your work," she suggested. "I may not be a master sorcerer, but I have some rather useful skills."

"Not unless you have experience binding essences," he replied.

The statement took Sirra by surprise, and she searched his face for any sign he was joking. "Are you serious?" she asked curiously.

He nodded once in reply and offered no explanation.

Taking a seat across from him, Sirra shook her head. "I should have known you'd be working on something so outlandish. You never stuck to conventional magic, that's for sure." She laughed quietly to herself.

"You're wasting my time," he said, the annoyance clear in his voice. "If you don't have anything to contribute, I'll be getting back to my work." He stood to leave, but Sirra grabbed his wrist.

"Wait," she said. "Perhaps I can be of some assistance to you." She patted the seat next to her, imploring him to sit.

"This had better be worth my time," he said as he sat.

"First off, whose essence are you trying to bind?"

"Yelaurad," he replied matter-of-factly.

"You can't be serious," she said, staring at him. No one had ever attempted binding a god, especially not the angry fire god Yelaurad. Such a task was unfathomable.

"Eventually, at least," he added upon seeing her dumbfounded expression.

"That would be monumental." Sirra had no idea that his ambitions reached so high. If such a thing were possible, she knew Telorithan would be the one to find a way. "Tell me how I can help," she said. "Or at least let me see what you've discovered."

"So far, I have practiced only on a single elf. The process was far simpler than I had imagined. The next step would be to trap something stronger, such as an elemental."

"We should travel to the Red Isle."

"I'm not ready for that," he admitted. "I have managed to bind an elf's power to augment my own, but he was weak. Before I attempt an elemental, I need to bind someone stronger."

"I see your point. Binding an elemental isn't going to be easy. They have immense power that we elves strive to emulate."

"Exactly. I should challenge a master sorcerer to a duel and bind his essence when he falls." Telorithan was sure he had the ability to beat any other sorcerer in battle.

"I know of something better than that," she replied as if dangling a carrot in front of him. Feeling as if she now had leverage, she decided to tease him a bit.

"Tell me," he demanded, his tone serious.

"Uh-uh," she said, wagging a finger near his nose. "Not so fast. I need something in return."

Telorithan stared at her, waiting for her to name her price. His arcane studies had focused intensely on fire and destruction, leaving no time to master the art of mind control. He regretted that fact momentarily, wishing he could drag the secret from her mind without having to play her silly games.

"I'd like a kiss first," she said provocatively.

He grabbed her and forcefully shoved his lips into hers. Holding a hand behind her head a little tighter than she would like, he continued the kiss as long as he could stand it before pushing her away.

"Now tell me."

"That wasn't a nice kiss," she said, the amusement draining from her face. "If you aren't going to play nice, I guess I'll have to keep what I know to myself."

Telorithan sighed and rolled his eyes. Why did she insist on acting like a child? There was no time for this. If she truly had useful information, she should share it without a fuss. He placed his hands on her cheeks and once again pulled her in for a kiss. This time he was gentle, and proceeded to kiss the side of her neck and shoulder as well.

"Is that better?" he asked.

"Much," she replied playfully. "There is an elf who is already bound by an elemental. If you bind him, you will almost certainly have the power to bind a full elemental."

Telorithan shot to his feet, staring at Sirra in disbelief. "Where is he? Why have I not heard of this?"

"Because you're too busy studying alone to pay attention to events happening around you," she replied. "I'll tell you where he is for another price." She drew the jeweled pin from her hair, allowing her raven locks to cascade freely about her shoulders. Her dark eyes narrowed, inviting him closer to her.

A wicked expression crept over his face as he grabbed her, pulling her body close to his. "You always know how to excite me."

Chapter 13

The waters of the Blue River danced and shimmered beneath the early-morning sunlight. Lenora had risen early and planned to have a walk beside the river and enjoy the beautiful weather. Her Coming of Age Ceremony would take place shortly after sunset, and she planned to savor her final day as an elf with no responsibilities. Tomorrow she would officially be an adult, and she would be expected to make her own place among her people.

As she arrived at the edge of the village, she removed her shoes and proceeded to the riverbank. She noticed River standing silently at the base of the waterfall, listening to the voice of the Spirit. A gentle mist had settled around him, but she could clearly make out his figure above the surface of the water. She smiled at the sight of him but chose not to disturb the interaction.

River was aware of her presence the moment her toes touched the water, yet his focus did not waver. He listened intently to the words of the Spirit.

A great evil has come upon the dwarves of the mountains. A presence resides in the water. To the village of stone you will travel, or many will surely die.

"What can I do for them?" River asked in earnest. "I would save the lives of those in danger, but I do not know what awaits me. How may I prepare?"

The magic you need awaits you there.

River waited for a few moments, hoping the Spirit would continue to speak. Though he could sense its presence moving away from him, he hoped it would return. He could not command the Spirit, and he still had questions about the dwarves. Today, it seemed, those questions would go unanswered.

Gliding through the clear waters, he stepped out onto the bank. Lenora still walked along the water's edge ahead of him. Wrapping himself in his robe, he walked quickly to catch her. It was not difficult to do, as her pace was slow and gentle.

"Good morning," he said from behind her.

She turned to see who had spoken and was pleased to see River approaching. As he drew closer, his sapphire-blue eyes preceded him, and she realized how handsome he truly was. She put the thought away for the moment and said, "Good morning."

"Might I walk with you a while?" he asked, his eyes pleading for her to say yes.

"Of course, my friend," she replied, turning to continue her course.

He strode along beside her, trying to think of an appropriate conversation. "Has your mother found out anything about the dwarf?"

"Unfortunately, no," she said. "She's thought of nothing except my Coming of Age Ceremony tonight."

"You must be excited," River replied.

"I am a little, I suppose," she said with a shrug. "There will be music and dancing, at least." She paused in her walking and turned to face River. "Will you be in attendance?"

"Only if you'll dance with me," he said, surprised by his own boldness.

"I'd love to." Her eyes twinkled with delight, and she looked down at the water to hide her smile. It surprised her how attracted she was to him. Her entire life had been spent studying magic and herbs. She'd had little time to make close friends, and she'd never before taken interest in a man. Perhaps she had put off her coming of age longer than she should.

"The Spirit of the river has said I'm to go into the mountains to a dwarf village," River said. "I think they need my help to cure the plague that has come upon them."

"Do you have skills as a healer?" she asked with much interest. It would certainly be something they had in common, and she wondered why he had not shared the fact with her before.

"Not really," he admitted. "The illness has something to do with the water, and that is most likely where I come in. Perhaps you could come along as a healer." His heart beat faster, hoping she would agree to accompany him. He dreaded that she might say no.

Pausing to consider his question, she finally replied, "I'd love to help, but please don't mention it to anyone else. I'll let my parents know tomorrow."

"We need to leave tomorrow," River said.

"I will tell them first thing." She knew they would protest, but she was of age and free to make her own decisions.

The pair turned around when they reached the edge of the forest and made their way slowly back to the village. There was little conversation between them, and they enjoyed the sounds of the Vale instead. Just being near Lenora was enough for River. He found himself struggling when he spoke to her anyway, so walking in silence was fine with him.

As they reached the village, River said, "I should let my father know about tomorrow."

Lenora nodded. "I'll see you tonight." With a smile, she turned and headed up the hill to her parents' home.

River approached his father's home in the silver tree and saw Galen waiting out front. "Afraid to wait inside?" he asked jokingly.

"Ryllak isn't exactly my first choice for fun conversation," Galen replied. "Anyway, I didn't have anything else to do."

"Aren't you supposed to be copying scrolls in the archives? It's required for your apprenticeship as a chronicler."

"Sometimes I have doubts about my choice of profession. The words themselves interest me more than the histories," he admitted.

"You want to write something else then?"

"No," Galen replied. "I think it's the words and letters themselves that I like."

"Maybe you should focus your attention on calligraphy," River suggested.

"Maybe," Galen said. "What have you been up to? I didn't see you by the waterfall."

"After I visited with the Spirit, I went for a walk with Lenora." His face lit up when he said her name.

"I see," Galen said, taunting his friend. "Did anything interesting take place? Anything you are dying to share the details of?" He grinned and nudged River with his elbow.

"Nothing," River said, shaking his head. "She does have her Coming of Age Ceremony tonight. She promised to dance with me."

"Nice," Galen replied, nodding his approval. "I'll tag along. I wouldn't want to miss a party."

"I need to speak with my father, so I'll see you later," River said. With a wave to his cousin, he stepped inside to find Ryllak sitting in his library.

"Father," he began, "I have some news."

Ryllak shut the book he was reading and motioned his son to have a seat. "You're leaving the Vale," he said.

"How did you know?" River asked as he took a seat next to his father.

"The look in your eyes. You've never been away, and you're afraid."

River looked down at the ground, ashamed of his apprehension. Never before had he traveled outside the Vale and the woods that surrounded it. A journey to the mountains may as well be a journey to the moon.

"Having fear does not make you a coward. Fear prevents us from jumping into things that could be dangerous. If the Spirit has given consent for this journey, then it is necessary for you to go. Doing what must be done despite your fear is what makes a person courageous."

River nodded, taking his father's words to heart. Ryllak always knew how to make him feel better, even when he had been singled out as a child. Ryllak had known his son was special and destined for great things. He accepted his role as River's father with great pride, and he hoped to guide him until his own journey came to an end.

Chapter 14

As Darvil was preparing to leave for town, he noticed a small group of dwarves crossing the field to his home. There were three of them, but from a distance he could not tell who they were. He rushed back to the farmhouse, hoping the men weren't looking for a fight. Kaiya's abilities were strange to him, but he knew she was capable of inflicting great harm. He had witnessed her powers occasionally as she practiced, and her magic was terrifyingly strong at times.

The three men paused outside the door to converse, giving Darvil the time he needed to reach them. He was relieved to recognize two councilmen, Anid and Gerry. They were known to him and had always been fair-minded dwarves. He was less pleased to see that Rudi, foreman of the mines, had come as well. Rudi was known to be a hothead, and he never seemed to know when to shut his mouth.

"Mornin'," Darvil said to the men. "What brings you out here?"

Anid stepped off the front porch first, a friendly smile on his lips. The majority of his face was hidden among fluffy white eyebrows and a partially tamed white beard. He reached out to shake Darvil's hand and said, "Good morning, Darvil. There's some trouble in town, and Rudi insisted we check with your girl about it. Gerry and me came to keep the peace."

"Where's the witch?" Rudi asked impatiently.

Darvil glared at the mine foreman. He was in no mood to listen to his daughter being insulted, especially on his own land.

"We don't need any of that," Gerry said, chiding the dwarf. "We're going to keep this civil." He reached for Darvil's hand as well, gripping it firmly and looking him in the eye. Gerry was a bit younger than Anid, and his yellow beard was well groomed and partially braided.

Hearing the voices outside, Kassie stepped out onto the porch, followed closely by Kaiya. Upon seeing the men, Kaiya knew they had come for her.

They did not frighten her, and she stepped in front of her mother, holding her head proudly in the air.

"You're here to speak to me, I take it." She stepped down from the porch and looked up at the three men. Rudi glared openly, not bothering to conceal his contempt for Kaiya.

"Perhaps we should all go inside and discuss a few things," Anid suggested.

"We can settle it here," Rudi grunted. "Take the spell off, witch, or else!" He was unarmed at the insistence of his companions, but he clenched his fists as he spoke.

"This one should learn to shut the hole in his face," Kaiya stated boldly. If these men had come for a fight, she would give them one they'd never forget. She had never used her magic to harm any living being, but to defend her family and her own life, she would not hold back.

"Let's not be hostile," Anid said, holding up both hands. "We want to speak to you is all. No one is here to hurt anyone."

"Kaiya," Gerry began, "you are the only person nearby with magic. We are hoping you can answer some questions for us, and then we will leave you in peace."

113

Kaiya looked to her mother, whose eyes were wide with apprehension. Darvil seemed more suspicious than nervous, but he nodded his approval to Kaiya.

"You can come in," he said, "but keep things civil."

Without another word, the three men headed inside the farmhouse, followed by Kaiya and her parents. Each of them took a seat around the kitchen table, the only place in the house big enough to hold everyone.

"Let me start off with a more thorough explanation," Gerry said. "Today the miners have not been able to enter the southwest facing cave. Anyone who enters is immediately attacked as if being strangled by an unseen hand."

Kassie gasped, putting her hands over her mouth. She stared at Gerry and did not look in Kaiya's direction.

"Six more dwarves have fallen ill, and there is still no sign of Jeb. He disappeared shortly after falling ill." Gerry searched Kaiya's expression for any hint that she knew something, but her face remained unchanging as he spoke.

"What does any of this have to do with my daughter?" Darvil asked, growing impatient.

Anid and Gerry exchanged glances.

"A cloaked figure was seen leaving the cave last night," Anid said. "It appeared to be a female."

"This is ridiculous," Darvil said, jumping to his feet.

Kaiya touched his arm to calm him, and he once again took his seat.

"It was me," Kaiya admitted. "I sensed the magic, and I thought I could help."

"I told you it was the witch!" Rudi pointed at Kaiya. "This girl is trouble. She's cursed the mine, and she needs to be punished!"

"You come near my daughter, and you won't live to tell about it." Darvil's brown eyes were serious as he glared at Rudi.

"We don't want any trouble here, and Rudi is not the one in charge," Anid said. "We came only to find out the truth so we might put our minds at ease. No one thinks Kaiya is a witch."

"Nor do we believe her capable of harming anyone," Gerry added.

"I went there to see if I could help," Kaiya declared. "That's all. There is an evil presence in the cave, and it is far stronger than me. I don't know how to get rid of it."

"If you do learn of anything that might help, Kaiya, please come to us first," Gerry said. "We don't want any misunderstandings, and your safety could be in jeopardy. Not everyone in our town is as open-minded as Anid and myself."

Kaiya nodded, trusting in the validity of his words. She would have to stay away from town indefinitely or risk getting into a fight with ignorant miners.

"Do you know any type of healing magic?" Anid asked. "So far there is no treatment to alleviate the miners' discomfort. Lives may be lost."

"I'm sorry, I do not know any healing magic," she said.

Medicine was not something that dwarves spent a lot of time studying. A man was either strong enough to overcome an illness on his own or he wasn't. They focused mainly on crude surgeries and folk remedies, most of which did little to help the sick. The women had a few effective remedies for their children, but those would prove inadequate against a magical illness.

The men rose to leave, and Darvil saw them to the door. Kaiya and Kassie remained seated, digesting the news about the miners.

As Darvil returned to the kitchen, he said, "I wish you'd give up this magic nonsense and settle down. There's going to be more trouble if this keeps up."

"I can't change what I am, Papa," Kaiya replied. "If I can find a way to help, I will do it. Magic is a part of me, and I would never give it up." She rose from her seat and headed to the door. Before she could depart, Darvil grabbed her arm and hugged her.

"It's you I care about," he said. "With or without magic, you're my little girl."

Chapter 15

Disappearing beneath the horizon, the sun bid farewell to the Vale. Myla was busy placing flowers in Lenora's hair while Albyn, Lenora's father, lit the blue magical fire that would illuminate the celebration throughout the evening. A variety of foods had been prepared, and the peach wine was already begging to flow. Nearly every adult elf in the Vale was in attendance to celebrate Lenora.

Lenora wore a shimmery white gown along with white flowers and ribbons upon her hair. As she stepped out among her kinsmen, they applauded and cheered. Her eyes danced over the crowd, searching the faces of those who had come to celebrate her special day. River was among them, dressed in a striking blue robe. Her eyes lingering on him for a moment, she felt herself begin to blush, and quickly turned her attention back to her parents.

Myla kissed her daughter on both cheeks and presented her with a gift. She hung a delicate silver medallion wrought with intricate vines around Lenora's neck before stepping back to admire her. Lenora ran a hand over the medallion's surface and pressed it to her heart.

"Thank you, Mother," she said, tears forming in her eyes. This was her grandmother's medallion, which Myla had received at her own Coming of Age Ceremony.

Next, Albyn stepped forward and kissed Lenora on her forehead. "May the goddess of the forest protect and keep you always."

In a crystalline soprano, Lenora lifted her voice in song. She sang sweetly of the elf maiden who transformed herself into a seabird and flew across the ocean, never to return. Her song had a hypnotic effect on River as he sat captivated by her voice. A single star appeared in the sky as she finished her song.

The crowd cheered for Lenora, and now the feast could commence. Though the inhabitants of the Vale did not consume the flesh of animals, there was still an abundance of savory foods to be found. The Vale's bounty of fruit and nuts provided a range of different flavors and options. The Westerling Elves were not opposed to sweets, as evidenced by the large number of dessert items.

Galen paid more attention to the food than anything. He sat at River's side, stuffing candies into his mouth. "Great party," he said through a mouthful of food.

River shook his head and turned his gaze back to Lenora. She sat next to her parents, enjoying some of the food herself. River found he had no appetite this evening. All of his thoughts focused on Lenora as he temporarily forgot about the next day's journey.

Some of the elves fired spells into the air, lighting the sky in a multitude of colors. The magic rained down upon the party, delighting the assembled guests. Musicians took the stage, playing stringed instruments and flutes while a slender white-haired elf sang in an elegant tone.

Galen, who had finally had his fill of eating, caught the eye of a chestnut-haired elf. She waved slightly with her fingers and flirted with her dark eyes. Grinning at River, Galen rose from his chair. "Looks like someone wants to dance," he declared. He made his way over to the lady and kissed her hand before leading her to the dance area.

River took a deep breath to calm his nerves. Lenora still sat between her parents, but he summoned his courage and headed her direction. Though her parents would disapprove, Lenora had promised him a dance. After all, she was an adult and capable of choosing a dance partner. Throwing his cares aside, he bravely stood before Lenora.

"May I have this dance, my lady?" he asked politely.

Myla and Albyn exchanged uneasy glances, but Lenora stood, ignoring their obvious displeasure.

"You certainly may," she replied, taking his hand.

Turning away from Lenora's parents, River said, "They seem less than pleased to see me."

"Don't worry about them," she replied. "They've forgotten what it was like to be young."

She slid her arm in his, and the two proceeded to the dance floor, where many elves were enjoying the fine music. Lenora wrapped her arms around River's neck, and he placed his hands upon her waist. They moved in time with the soft strumming of a harp, occasionally looking into each other's eyes. Though he felt shy and awkward at first, River finally managed to relax and enjoy the moment.

When the music came to an end, Lenora said, "That was lovely."

"I'm afraid I'm not much of a dancer," he admitted.

"This is a perfect time to learn," she replied, taking his hand once again.

The music switched to a faster pace, and she led him into the group of dancing elves. They danced as one unit, switching partners and clapping their hands. Though many of them took less-than-perfect steps, a good time was had by all.

Shortly after midnight, the crowd began to disperse. Lenora's parents had already retired for the night, and she had spent her time in River's company without their condescending looks.

Taking one last sip of peach wine, Lenora said, "I guess we should get some sleep. We have a big day ahead of us tomorrow."

Though many of the flowers had fallen from her hair and she seemed tired from all the dancing, Lenora still looked as radiant as ever to River. Her pale eyes reflected the moonlight, and her white gown glowed as if by magic.

"I suppose so," he replied. He was reluctant to leave her side, even for one night.

Galen joined them as they were saying their goodbyes, throwing an arm around each of them. The smell of peach wine was strong on his breath. "I've decided," he said, looking at River. "I'm going to the mountains with you tomorrow. I've always had an affinity for rocks."

"The more the merrier," Lenora replied.

"You're going?" Galen asked, surprised.

"Yes," she replied with a smile. "The dwarves are in need of a healer."

"Well, then," he began, "we'll be in fine company."

"Indeed we will," River replied, still gazing at Lenora.

The clouds rolled in, leaving the Vale in darkness as the trio departed to rest. The next day would bring them to an unfamiliar place, where an evil presence awaited them. This night would be spent in safety, but the future was uncertain.

Chapter 16

Books and scrolls went flying through the air as Telorithan searched the contents of his library. His immense collection of documents was another thing he took pride in. Somewhere within these items he would find the spell necessary to allow him to track the elemental living in the Westerling Vale.

Two servants scrambled to pick up each scroll and volume as it landed. Any damage to these items would be blamed on them, regardless of who was truly responsible. They stacked the books carefully, hoping to avoid a large pileup. If their master's path was obstructed as he moved about the library, he would be rather unhappy. Facing Telorithan's anger was not something the servants wished to do this day.

Pulling out a dust-covered tome, Telorithan sneezed loudly. Turning to the servants, he asked, "Is it too difficult for you to keep this place clean?"

The two servants looked at each other nervously and hung their heads without responding.

Rising from his knees with the book in hand, he said, "I expect this room to be spotless when I return, or the two of you will be melted down into something useful."

The pair frantically set about cleaning to rid the library of dust. Telorithan was a man of his word, and his threats were always taken seriously.

Exiting the library, Telorithan ascended the spiral staircase to his laboratory. He laid the book open on a long wooden table and flipped through its pages. This book was one of only five copies in existence of a five-thousand-year-old tome authored by Master Zarthan, the most proficient scryer in history. If anyone had a method for tracking an elemental, it would be him.

Failing to find the information he sought on the first look, he slammed his fist against the table in frustration. He turned away from the book and faced the fireplace behind him. With a casual movement of his finger, a fire roared to life within the hearth. As he stared into the flames, he realized he had been searching for the wrong thing. He did not need a new method to track the movements of an elemental. It would be simpler to find one using fire. Having mastered the flames many years ago, he had used them to communicate in the past. Chuckling slightly to himself, he realized how simple the task before him would be.

Flipping through the tome's pages once again, he found a section entitled *Scrying with Fire*. All that was required, besides his own power, were a few cinders from the Red Isle, a gemstone, and an item to represent the person being viewed. The cinders were simple, as he always kept those on hand for various magical purposes. Obviously, the gemstone would be a sapphire. No other gem would suffice for finding a water elemental. A moment's thought was all he needed to decide on a third item: a small piece of driftwood from the shore near his tower would work perfectly. An object that had spent countless days adrift in the blue would hold enough water memory to serve his purpose.

His final hurdle would be conquering the distance. The Westerling Vale was not only across the sea, but it was also a few days' journey across land. Not to mention it was blocked on one side by mountains and the other by a river. These obstacles would make the magic harder to achieve. He was undeterred, however, and confident in his own abilities.

Touching his hand to a small brass sphere on his mantle, he summoned a servant to his side. With all speed, the elf ran to the laboratory.

"I require a piece of driftwood," Telorithan commanded.

"Right away, Master," the elf replied, before running back down the stairs.

The far end of the laboratory was stocked with ingredients and various items that were used in Telorithan's experiments. From one of his many coffers, he chose a small sapphire to feed to the flames. After a short search, he recovered a glass container full of ash from the Red Isle. These were the remains of magic created by the most spectacular fire elementals in all Nōl'Deron. They had unique properties, which were required for various spells and held a substantial amount of power. If this practice session with a water elemental succeeded, he would try his hand at binding a fire elemental next. That was the power he longed for.

The servant returned with a foot-long piece of driftwood, and he bowed as he presented it to his master. Snatching the item from the servant's hand, Telorithan turned his attention back to the fireplace. The servant backed away slowly, expecting no gratitude to be expressed by his master. He took a position near the door, in case Telorithan required further assistance.

Telorithan methodically added the items to the fire, all the while muttering an inaudible incantation. The flames danced and sputtered as they received the offering. A soft orange glow filled the room, a sign that the spell was working.

Holding one hand to his forehead and extending the other toward the fire, Telorithan closed his eyes and projected his mind into the flames. As he opened his eyes, he saw the land outside his home pass by, and the ocean appeared before him. He flew with a bird's-eye view of the sea, passing waves and sea spray, until he once again reached land. The landscape passed by but soon faded. The fire would require more magic to see farther into the distance.

The smooth amethyst that contained the essence of the murdered thief sat idly in Telorithan's pocket. Drawing it up to his eye, he peered at the elf trapped inside. A mist swirled within, taking the shape of the dead man's face. His eyes pleaded with the master sorcerer to release him from his torment. Without a thought for the imprisoned elf's suffering, Telorithan flung the gem into the fire. The thief's power was now a part of the spell.

Focusing on the flames once again, the image of the land became clearer. He passed the edge of the Wrathful Mountains and into the forest that surrounded the Vale. The sapphire in the flames began to spin, giving a blue coloration to the fire. To Telorithan's disappointment, the Vale was impenetrable. A force resided there that was too powerful to be spied upon. The Spirit protected the Westerling Elves from all harm, and Telorithan would not be able to penetrate its defenses from this distance.

Telorithan continued past the Vale and into the mountains above. A dwarven village came into view, and he felt the presence of great magic there. This was a curious discovery, as he had never heard of dwarves practicing any type of magic except rune carving. He wondered if perhaps there was an earth elemental dwelling among the mountains.

Ending the spell, Telorithan took a seat near the window and stared out over the sea. At the very least, he knew the spell had worked. The elemental elf was still present in the Vale. He would either have to go there and lure it out, or he would have to wait for it to journey from the protected area. Neither scenario seemed likely. Given the power of the Westerling Elves, he could not hope to subdue them all long enough to drag the elemental away. There was a slim chance the elf would leave the area, but he would have to stay near a vast supply of water in order to maintain his power.

Not yet willing to give up on the idea, he started to devise a new plan. Surely within his library was information that could help. He also had the entire university and some powerful friends that he could coerce into helping him. The matter was not yet settled. He would have this elemental's power added to his own.

Chapter 17

A bright morning arrived in the Vale, lighting River's path to consult with the Spirit. Disrobing at the edge of the water, he dove into the depths of the Blue River. Emerging near the base of the waterfall, he focused his mind into the water to summon the Spirit within. Today he would travel into the mountains, and he was eager for the Spirit's guidance.

To his disappointment, the Spirit did not appear. There was no vision, and he was given no instructions on how to proceed. A solitary line repeated in his ears: *the magic you need awaits you there.* Perhaps that meant he was to use the entity's magic against itself. Without further explanation, he was unsure whether he was correct.

Feeling burdened and uncertain, he returned to the riverbank and retrieved his clothing. Today he had chosen a fine blue robe, embroidered with silver vines. When he encountered the dwarves, he hoped he would make a good impression. He did not intend to appear before them as a wanderer but rather as a dignified elf who had come to offer assistance.

Ryllak waited a few steps beyond the hill that led down to the river. He could already see the look of disappointment on his son's face as he returned from the water. Ryllak had also hoped the Spirit would offer more guidance today, but it appeared that was not the case. River shook his head as he reached his father, affirming that he had received no message.

"It isn't needed then," Ryllak said reassuringly. "You will know what to do when it needs to be done."

Still unsure, River could only hope his father was correct.

Lenora stepped outside, followed closely by her parents. Tossing a cloth bag full of herbs and medicines over one shoulder, she walked across the village to meet her traveling companions.

"Lenora, this is too dangerous!" Albyn insisted, trying his best to keep pace with his daughter.

"Please listen," her mother pleaded. "You don't know this elf you're leaving with. Your life could be in danger."

Pausing with a huff, Lenora turned to face her mother. "He's not going to kill me, Mother. You don't even know him, so how can you judge? I'm going to do what I can for the dwarves." Spinning on her heels, she continued on her way. Her parents remained silent but continued to follow until she reached River and Ryllak.

"You're all right with this?" Albyn asked Ryllak. "This isn't proper behavior for two young elves."

"They are of age," Ryllak said dismissively. "They choose their own paths."

"If any harm comes to my daughter, I'm holding you responsible." Myla looked at River as she spoke, her eyes conveying the truth behind her words. She did not trust him, but she could no longer control her daughter.

Lenora shook her head, trying her best to ignore her parents. "Good morning, Lord Ryllak, River," she said, nodding to each of them. "I'm all set to go."

"We're still missing Galen," River replied.

"No you're not!" Galen's voice called.

The elves looked around but saw no sign of him.

"There," Lenora said, pointing into the village.

Galen was hurrying to their meeting place, still stuffing fruit into a bag. "We can't go without food," he said as he reached them. "Who knows what dwarves eat?" He looked around at the assembled elves and clamped his mouth shut. Lenora's parents appeared almost comical, trailing after their grown daughter. Ryllak had his usual worried look that had tempted Galen more than once to try making the elf laugh. Today, he decided to behave properly and resist the urge to make jokes about his elders.

"I think it's time we were underway," River suggested.

"I'm all set," Galen chimed in. "How are we planning to get up that mountain? Do you have wings hiding under that robe?"

Ryllak sighed at Galen's cheeky comment. "You're going to climb and lower a rope for the other two."

"Oh!" Galen said, taken aback. "So, he does have a sense of humor."

Ryllak's lips quivered, suppressing a smile. This was a serious situation, and a little bit of humor could only help to lighten the mood.

"I can get us up the mountain easily," River said. "Are you ready?" he asked Lenora.

"I am," she stated firmly.

"Lenora—" her mother began.

"I'm going, Mother," she replied, cutting her off. "I can take care of myself."

Myla stepped back, leaning against her life-mate. "Be well, my daughter," she said, tears welling in her eyes.

"Take care of her," Albyn said to River, his tone serious.

"Of course," River replied. He turned to his companions and said, "We're going to travel up the waterfall. You might get a bit wet."

Galen and Lenora exchanged worried looks. Neither of them had traveled in that fashion, and they weren't sure what to expect.

"It's quite safe," River said with a smile. The trio headed down to the riverbank and made their way along the edge of the water until they came near the waterfall. River stepped into the water first, bidding his friends to wait on dry land.

Placing both hands at the surface of the water, River bowed his head and focused energy into the water. Before their eyes, the waterfall ceased to flow, forming itself into a tall flight of steps. A path stretched from the stairs to the bank, allowing Lenora and Galen to follow without having to swim.

The pair looked at River in amazement as he emerged once again from the water.

"Follow me," River said. Leading the way, he moved along the path to the stairs.

Galen and Lenora stepped forward onto the solid path as the water continued to flow all around them. This was magic never before seen in the Vale. The path was neither frozen nor slippery. The water had simply transformed into a solid path before their eyes.

Ryllak had followed from a distance, his mind full of worry as well as hope. His only son was leaving the safety of the Vale for the first time. There was no way to know what he would encounter, and he could no longer protect him from harm.

As the three friends reached the stairway, River turned to see his father standing on the bank. Ryllak raised a hand, saying farewell to his son. River waved back and also sent a ripple through the water that splashed around Ryllak's feet. He knew his father would worry, even though River had assured him he would be safe. River was too young to yet understand the emotion that goes along with being a parent.

Lenora followed behind River as they climbed the stairs, and Galen took up a position behind her.

"I shall catch you if you fall, beautiful lady," he declared with a chuckle.

"That's actually not all that comforting," she replied. To River, she asked, "Couldn't you have fashioned a hand rail for these stairs?"

River turned back to look at her feeling slightly embarrassed. "I hadn't thought of it," he admitted.

"Use the rocks," Galen stated, slapping his hand against a slippery black rock.

"Thanks for the suggestion," Lenora said sarcastically. Looking up, she added, "We're almost to the top."

River stepped up onto the plateau and extended a hand to Lenora. Once the three of them were safely above the falls, they looked down over the Vale.

"I never thought I'd see home from this angle," Lenora admitted. She jumped in surprise as River released the spell, allowing the waterfall to flow freely once more.

Galen, who had been splashed by the rushing waters, said, "Thanks for the warning."

Chapter 18

Kaiya sat idly upon a boulder at the outskirts of her family's farm. The wind caressed her face and tousled her short hair as it swept past and changed directions. In the palm of her hand, she summoned sparks and shaped them into spheres before allowing them to float freely on the wind. She still did not know how to banish the evil presence from the cave, but she remained determined to do so. There had to be a way, and if she listened to the wind long enough, perhaps it would whisper the answer.

She spun around to face a rocky ledge and lifted her face to the wind. *Someone is coming.* She opened her eyes and looked around but saw no one. The feeling was unmistakable. A being of magic was drawing near. It was not the malevolent force from the cave, however.

This was something entirely different. Her curiosity encouraged her to move closer to the ledge and see who was there.

Lying flat on her stomach to avoid being seen, she peered down from the top of the ledge. No one was there. Sitting back up on her knees, she again closed her eyes and tried to sense the magical creature. It was nearby and moving in her direction. She could hear voices in the distance before catching a glimpse of three figures approaching along the trail below. They drew ever nearer but did not look to the ledge above them. Kaiya could see that they were elves, and she was surprised by the strength of the magic she sensed in them.

"Umm, hello," she said as they came closer.

At the sound of her voice, the three elves stopped walking and looked up. On the ledge above them was Kaiya, peering cheerfully down at them.

"Hello, my lady," River said.

Kaiya chuckled. She couldn't recall ever being addressed in such a way. "Are you lost?"

"Actually, I think we've found what we're looking for," River said, a smile spreading across his face. He looked into Kaiya's gray eyes and saw her magic. "We are seeking the dwarf village that lies above the Vale, and it seems as though we've found it."

"Not quite," she replied. "You've found me, though, and I can lead you to the village."

River gave Lenora a boost to climb over the rocks leading up to Kaiya's level. Galen followed second, and River came quickly behind him.

Brushing the dirt from her dress, Lenora looked at Kaiya with great interest. Her hair was a deep purple, and though she stood only to the height of River's waist, she was proportionate and finely shaped. She was curvier than the average elf woman with wide hips and a strong build. "You're lovely!" Lenora exclaimed.

A surprised Kaiya looked back at her. "Thank you," she said, not sure if she should be offended.

"Forgive me, I didn't mean to sound surprised by your looks. I've never seen a dwarf woman before. I suppose I had pictured your kind differently." She looked down at her feet, shuffling slightly.

"It's all right," Kaiya replied. "I see three elves before me, and I can feel magic in all of you." She moved closer to River. "You are not entirely elf, I think. Your magic feels different than the other two."

"That's correct," he said. "I am also a water elemental."

"Do you know of an air elemental?" she asked eagerly.

"There are none in the Vale," he replied. "I do sense air magic in you. Perhaps you could summon one for both of us." He looked into her eyes knowingly, and she looked away to avoid his sapphire gaze.

"It's silly, I know, but I hear things on the wind from time to time," she said. "It has helped me to focus my magic."

"I didn't know dwarves practiced any magic," Galen said.

"Most don't," she replied. "I am the only one around here who does."

"How did you learn?" he asked.

"I've taught myself, for the most part," she said. "I do have an old book my father bought from a peddler, but it hasn't been much help."

"I think you have learned more from the wind than any book could teach," River said. "Yours is not the kind of magic that can be taught. Instead, it lives within you, and you are the one who must figure out how to wield it. We are more alike than you realize."

Kaiya did not fully understand his words. She had practiced alone her whole life and would welcome the chance to have formal training. It seemed these elves would not be much help with that. "Why did you come here?" she asked.

"We've been told of a sickness that is plaguing the dwarves in this area," Lenora said. "You look perfectly healthy though."

Kaiya blushed. She was not used to receiving so many compliments. "There is illness among the miners," she began. "There is a dark presence within one of the mining caves, and I believe it is making the men ill."

"Have you seen this presence?" River asked.

"I have," she admitted. "I went inside the cave to figure out what was going on. I saw the apparition of an elf woman, and she attacked me. There was nothing I could do to stop her."

Galen's eyes went wide. "Do you think she means to kill them?"

"She's already killed one," River replied. "We have to find out why she is here and how we can convince her to leave."

"What do you mean she has already killed?" Kaiya asked, her eyes showing concern. "I know of no one dying from this sickness."

"Forgive me," River said. "The body of one of your kinsmen came over the waterfall into the Vale. That is how I knew you needed help."

"Jeb," she whispered. "He was missing." Though she had not known him well, Kaiya's heart sank for Jeb's family. "We have to stop this before others are lost." Determination replaced her sorrow. "I will take you to the village. Don't expect them to be welcoming. They are ignorant when it comes to magic, and some of them think I had a hand in this."

"Did you?" Galen asked.

"No," she replied, shocked by the question. "Of course I didn't."

"Good," he replied. "Now that we've gotten that question out of the way, we can all be friends." He smiled and laid a hand on her shoulder. "Lead on."

She shook her head, realizing that Galen had not meant any offense. "Only a few of my kinsmen have seen elves before. This meeting could be interesting."

"Let's hope it isn't disastrous," Galen said, laughing.

Galen had no idea how correct his statement might prove. The dwarves of Kaiya's village had no use for magic, and three magical beings appearing in this time of fear might lead to trouble.

Chapter 19

Leading the elves across the green field, Kaiya

traveled at an easy pace. She was not in a hurry to encounter the townsfolk, and she knew the elves could not expect a warm welcome. She pointed to the farmhouse as they passed by. "I live there," she told them.

"It's a lovely home," Lenora commented, stepping forward to walk next to Kaiya.

Doozle spotted the group from a distance and ran toward them, bounding over the tall stalks of prairie grass. His mouth was open, giving the best doggish smile he could manage. The group paused, allowing him to sniff at them until he was content.

River knelt to stroke the dog's soft fur. "Aren't you a friendly one?" he asked.

Doozle sat proudly and barked once in response.

Kaiya hugged the happy dog and said, "You have to stay here, Doozle. There could be trouble, and I don't want you in the middle of it."

Doozle whined softly, his eyes begging to join his friend.

"Not this time," she said, shaking her head. "Go to Papa in the fields," she commanded, pointing. "Go on."

With one bark, Doozle turned and headed back across the field.

"Do elves have dogs?" she asked curiously.

Lenora replied, "We have only the animals of the forest. They live freely and don't need us to care for them."

"I suppose that's nice," she said. "You might be missing out though." Kaiya couldn't imagine not having Doozle around. He'd been her companion for many years.

They continued along the path until they reached the village. The blacksmith's hammer was already audible in the distance, ringing in time with their steps. It was nearly midday, and the town was alive with activity. Kaiya hoped that most of the miners had found work in a different cave for the time being. She didn't want to have too large a crowd greeting them as they entered the village.·

At the edge of town, Kaiya could see a large tent had been set up near the marketplace. "That must be where they're keeping the sick," she said.

"Lenora is a healer," Galen said, noticing Kaiya's concerned expression.

"I'll do whatever I can to help them," Lenora said reassuringly.

"This is a magical illness," Kaiya replied. "If we can convince the spirit to leave, or at least reverse the spell she has cast, then the illness will cease to spread."

"That's going to be River's area of expertise," Galen said. "I'm only here for a change of scenery."

Kaiya eyed him suspiciously. "I think you've come seeking something else," she said.

Galen shrugged and stared off into the distance.

"I have been told this illness has to do with the water," River said. "In that case, I should be able to help." His words sounded confident. Being sent by the Spirit, River felt certain he would succeed in the task before him.

"Who told you that?" Kaiya asked.

Smiling, he replied, "The water that has its source in the mountains creates the river that runs through the Vale. It has a voice, as does the wind."

Kaiya understood what he meant. "If the water speaks to you, perhaps it can tell you how to be rid of this presence. I don't think I have the strength to banish her."

"I do not know what it will require, but once I've spoken with her, perhaps an answer will reveal itself."

As they moved to the center of the village, all activity ceased. Every pair of eyes in the town looked upon the three elves and Kaiya. Such a spectacle had not been seen among their kind in recent memory. Kaiya steeled herself against an attack. She felt her magic pulsing through her veins, ready to defend her new friends.

A group of dwarves circled around to have a better look at the visitors. Many of them pointed and whispered to each other. Kaiya stood with her hands on her hips, waiting for someone to begin an argument. She wouldn't have to wait long. Rudi pushed his way to the front of the crowd.

"Look what we have here. It's the witch and some pointy-eared forest dwellers," Rudi said mockingly.

"They've come here to help you," Kaiya spat back. "You should show them a little courtesy, but I see you're incapable."

River stepped forward, hoping to stop the argument from escalating. "Please," he began, "we wish only to help." He laid a hand on Lenora's arm. "This is Lenora, a skilled healer. She will help tend to your men. I will help you rid yourselves of the evil presence in the cave."

Rudi was unmoved by River's words. "Tell that witch to take the curse off, elf man, and we'll be fine."

Kaiya held back her temper, not wanting to make the situation worse. She was relieved to see Ortin coming forward to help. He was followed by Trin, the town's rune carver. Both men clutched hammers in their hands.

"All right, that's enough out of you," Ortin said. "They've come all this way to help, so let them help."

"Stay out of this, blacksmith," Rudi said, clenching his fists.

"That'll be quite enough, Rudi," Trin said, tapping his hammer against his hand.

"You better watch it, old man," Rudi replied, the blood rising to his face.

"Clear out, all of you!" Trin demanded.

The crowd dispersed at his request. Trin was highly respected among the townsfolk, and they were content to obey him. Rudi, however, did not budge.

"You don't frighten me, rune carver," he said. "Just because you dabble in magic charms doesn't make you a wizard."

"You're right," he replied. "I don't use magic, but I'll carve my name into your face if you don't get out of here." He took an aggressive step forward, and Rudi backed away.

"This isn't over," Rudi said as he walked away. He did not go far before turning to observe the elves again. If they were going into his mine, he would be there to watch.

Kaiya introduced the elves to the two dwarf men. "The elves are here to help us," she declared.

"It's a pleasure," Ortin said, extending a hand to each of them. "Name's Ortin, and this here is Trin."

"I never thought I'd see an elf," Trin said. A stout man with a long silver beard, Trin was not usually one to stand in awe. Today, though, he could not help being intrigued by them.

"You're a rune carver?" Galen asked.

"I am indeed," he replied. "The men of my family have been rune carvers for seven generations."

"Fascinating," Galen said, his eyes sparkling. "I'd love to see your work."

"Follow me," Trin replied, anxious to show his skill to the elf.

"I should see to the ill," Lenora said.

"I'll take you to the hospital tent," Ortin said. "They've set up outside the cave to keep everyone together."

Inside the tent were nearly thirty sick dwarves. Only one physician tended them, and the patients were clearly still in pain. They were restless in their beds, most of them shivering or moaning.

"The illness grows worse daily," Ortin said.

"I shall do what I can," Lenora declared. She left them behind to speak with the doctor.

"Let's get you over to the cave, shall we?" Ortin said to River.

"Certainly," he replied.

The cave was only a few hundred feet from the medical tent. River had sensed dark magic since entering the town, but it grew stronger as he neared the cave. Ortin stopped outside and motioned River to go ahead.

"I'll wait out here," he said.

"Good luck," Kaiya said, choosing to remain outside as well. She doubted she could be much help to someone as powerful as River. All of her senses told her he was strong, and she hoped he would prevail easily against the apparition.

River stepped inside and immediately felt a heaviness in his chest. Undeterred, he pressed on until he came to a clear pool of water where he could sense the source of the magic.

"Show yourself," he commanded. Immediately, he felt as if a hand were trying to grip his throat. He fought back with magic, not allowing the evil spirit to frighten him.

The image of an elf woman appeared before him. "You are a strange being," she said. "I can sense your power, but you are not strong enough to command me."

"I have come to help you," he replied. "Tell me what I can do."

"You can leave this place and never return!"

With those words, she sent out a magical blast that knocked River backward. As soon as he regained his footing, she sent out a second blast, this time strong enough to expel him from the cave. He flew out into the light, landing hard on his backside.

154

The sound of the first blast had attracted a crowd, which arrived in time to witness the event. Lenora and Galen both heard the noise and came to check on their friend. Seeing him fly out of the cave backward was unexpected, and they rushed to his aid.

"Are you all right?" Lenora asked, scanning his body with white magic.

Seeing that his friend was conscious, Galen said, "Why didn't you summon a puddle to cushion your fall?" He chuckled, not bothering to hide his amusement.

River stared at him, his expression one of annoyance.

The dwarves muttered among themselves, but one voice came through loud and clear. Rudi laughed heartily and said, "Look at me! I'm a magical elf man, and I've come to save the day." He doubled over laughing and slapped his hand against his knee. Turning away from the incident, he wiped tears from his eyes. The other dwarves joined him in laughing for a moment before returning to their own affairs.

"It would seem only your pride is wounded," Lenora declared, finishing her scan. She tucked in her lips to suppress a giggle.

Galen continued to laugh, and Kaiya stared at River, wondering if he would have the power necessary to force the apparition to leave. She knew the evil creature was capable of great magic, but she had hoped River would prove stronger. It would seem he had his limits as well, and it was clear they would need to work together.

River finally stood, rubbing his lower back. "She's more powerful than I expected."

Kaiya nodded. "Now you see what we're up against."

Chapter 20

Gazing into the fire, Telorithan watched as River left the protection of the Vale and journeyed into the mountains. *He's making this too easy*, he thought. A heaviness came over him as he continued to observe the elf, and he sensed an additional magical being was nearby. Neither dwarves nor Westerling Elves naturally possessed the level of magic he felt emanating from the fire. It rivaled the power of an elemental, and his own power as well. Telorithan felt uneasy, not knowing what dwelt in the mountains.

Perhaps he is there to meet with an earth elemental. The idea of taking on two elementals, even with one of them being in elf form, did not sit well with him. It was rare for him to doubt his abilities, but this was magic he had never yet attempted. He knew he could best any Enlightened Elf who was foolish enough to challenge him, but the power of an elemental is raw and untamed. In the back of his mind, he wondered if he had the strength to conquer one.

A soft knock came from the laboratory door, and a servant slowly poked his head inside. "Sirra is here to see you, Master," he said quietly.

"Show her in," he replied without looking at the servant.

Sirra could be rather annoying, but she was also quite intelligent. If she could assist him in further augmenting his powers, then she might be worth his time. A cleverer enchantress he had never met, especially considering the difficulty women had in learning magic. Enlightened Elf women were never granted the title of Master, since they were not given the proper training to master any portion of the craft. Sirra had immense talent, but she could never hope to be as powerful as a man. A woman's training was capped at one hundred years, while men were allowed to study indefinitely.

"Hello, dear," Sirra said as she entered the room. She leaned in to kiss a grimacing Telorithan on his cheek. "What are you looking at in the fire?"

"The elemental you told me about," he replied, without looking away from the fire.

"I see," she replied, gazing into the flames. "How do you plan to subdue him? Will you gather an army to invade the Vale?"

"He's no longer in the Vale. He's traveled into the mountains to a dwarf village."

Sirra laughed. "What could he possibly want from them?"

"I know not," he replied. "They are ignorant of all things magic and unworthy of my time. There must be something other than dwarves that has drawn the elemental's attention."

"At least dwarves will be easily conquered, being without magic themselves. You won't have anything to worry about."

Telorithan turned to look at her, his eyes severe. "There is magic there unlike any that should be present among the dwarves. I believe there may be a second elemental."

Sirra's eyes went wide. This was exciting news, and she briefly thought he might ask for her help. His pride would prevent him from asking directly, but perhaps she could offer in a way that would not insult him. Now would not be the best time to offer, but once he had a plan in place, she could more easily offer her assistance. The once-in-a-lifetime chance of being present at the binding of an elemental was something she simply had to witness.

"Do you mean you could capture two of them?" she asked, her excitement building.

"I don't know," he said, turning away. He would never reveal his reservations about taking on one elemental, let alone two.

Staring deep into the fire, Sirra said, "I sense the ancient magic of an elemental, but also something else."

"A second elemental?" he asked eagerly.

"No, this is much younger. It is no less wild, though. I would say it is someone powerful yet untested." She gave Telorithan a sly look. "You might be the right elf to test it."

He scoffed at her, knowing her words to be pure flattery. "Don't bother me with your flirtations. Take them elsewhere if you can't be of assistance."

"It looks like they're heading for a cave. You won't be able to sense anything in there."

"You doubt my abilities?"

"Not at all," she replied. "Surely you remember some earth magic from before your studies with fire. The metals in the cave will prevent scrying."

Telorithan had long since forgotten some basic elemental magic. His focus had rested purely with fire and learning new ways to harness its power. "Remembering that sort of thing is beneath me," he said with a dismissing wave of his hand. She was correct. Once the elemental entered the cave, he could no longer sense it. The other presence, however, was still just as strong. *Whatever the other being is, it is not inside that cave.* Looking more closely, Telorithan could see no one but dwarves. In his eyes, they were incapable of any real magic, so he dismissed them without a second thought.

"Come away from this," Sirra begged. "Let's pass the time in a more enjoyable manner."

"Nothing could be more enjoyable," he said. "I am nearing my ultimate goal of binding a god. What could be better?"

"What would you do with all that power?" Her voice sounded playful.

"Firstly, I would live apart from those who annoy me." His eyes narrowed as he looked at her.

161

"Well, I have in mind something that you're better at than magic." She brushed her fingers through his silver hair and licked her lips seductively.

As his anger rose, Telorithan's eyes flashed red. "I am better at nothing than magic. Get out of my sight," he commanded, pointing to the door.

Obviously hurt, she replied, "But, I only meant—"

"I said leave!" he shouted, before turning his back to her.

With a sigh, she turned to leave. Without looking back, she slammed the door behind her. Telorithan ignored the sound and gazed deeper into the flames. Before his eyes, the elemental was forced from the cave, landing unceremoniously on his behind. Laughing quietly to himself, he thought, *This one might not be as strong as I feared.*

Chapter 21

Stepping closer to the cave and peering inside, Kaiya

said, "I'll go in with you this time." She regretted not going with him the first time. Her magic may well have protected him from the attack, and she wouldn't let him go alone again.

River nodded, looking down at the young dwarf. He admired her determination and courage. She had already felt this being's wrath and witnessed her attack on River, but she did not hesitate to venture back inside.

"We'll all come," Lenora said, stepping forward.

Galen looked uneasily at her. Facing down a magical being that could best River was not something he hoped to do.

"Thank you, Lenora, but you two should wait outside. I don't want to overwhelm whoever this apparition is. It's best if only Kaiya and I enter."

Galen let out a breath in relief.

"All right, but if I hear anything that concerns me, I'm coming in." Lenora trusted his judgment, but she wouldn't stand by while others were hurt. She might not be able to match the power of the being within the cave, but she would do whatever was necessary to help her friends.

Kaiya stepped inside with River, and the two disappeared in the darkness. A chill ran up Kaiya's spine, but still she pressed on. River seemed unfazed as they journeyed deeper inside. A cold wind blew as they neared the gleaming white basin that lay directly in front of the apparition's pool. The sound of rushing water filled their ears and invigorated River. Closing his eyes, he approached the water cascading from the cave ceiling. Cupping his hands, he collected some water and rubbed it onto his face. His eyes flashed with blue fire.

A sense of calm came over Kaiya. Before she had felt only anger within the cave, but now she could sense peace and serenity. River's magic was overwhelming the hatred and replacing it with kindness. The wind swirled as a light appeared over the pool. Kaiya realized this was her chance to prepare, and she threw out her arms to gather the wind about her. Laying her hands on top of her heart, she closed her eyes and ignored the light forming before her. Focusing only on the wind itself, she created a shield to protect her from the evil spirit's attack. A swirling vortex of wind surrounded her, and her eyes glowed with a silver light.

Side by side, River and Kaiya faced the apparition. This time, she would not force them from the cave.

"Why have you come to this place?" River asked.

The elf spirit reached out her hand, testing the layers of magic surrounding her visitors. Finding it respectably strong, she said, "You are not the beings who came before me previously. Now you show your true forms."

Kaiya remained focused, refusing to allow the spirit's words to distract her. Any lapse in concentration and her spell of protection might fail. "You are harming my kinsmen," she said. "You must stop."

The apparition laughed, throwing her arms up in the air. "Wind and water, such a brave pair," she said, still laughing.

A bright flash of light blinked before their eyes, but still their magic held fast. The cave rumbled, and rocks fell from the ceiling. Projecting his aura of peace, River refused to be moved by her tricks. Kaiya tensed momentarily but opened her mind to absorb the calm of her companion. Without River at her side, she knew her concentration would fail. Her eyes filled with tears, wishing she could express her gratitude.

"You will not drive us away," River said. "I can sense your torment, and I would help you if I could. Tell us how we can free you from this place."

"You wish only to expel me!" she cried, her voice filling with anger.

A blue light emitted from River's hand and slowly made its way to the apparition. Screaming with rage at its approach, the woman held up a hand to block it. Undeterred, the blue light encompassed her, calming her despite her efforts to stop it. Tears glistened as they slowly slid down her cheeks, and an immense sadness filled the cave.

Kaiya felt herself beginning to falter, and she dropped to one knee. Bowing her head, she once again tried to focus her mind to hold the spell. River placed his hand on her shoulder, his aura once again giving her strength. The sadness did not disappear, but

166

Kaiya's heart was lifted. She stood strong once more, the air continuing to swirl around her.

Turning his attention back to the apparition, River saw her tears. "Let us help you," he said quietly.

"You cannot help," she replied. "I am bound to this place."

"There is a way to free you, and we will find it," he said.

"I was murdered here," she stated. "The one I loved most betrayed me, and now I cannot leave. I have slept here for many long years, but the dwarves have disturbed my rest. They must be punished."

"My people meant you no harm," Kaiya said. "They are ignorant of magic, and they did not feel your presence."

The apparition's eyes filled with anger at Kaiya's response. "You could sense me," she spat. "You should have stopped them."

"They don't listen to me," Kaiya replied. "They fear magic."

"Then they deserve their fate," she declared.

"I am sorry they disturbed you," Kaiya continued. "They were unaware, and they don't deserve what you've done to them. Please let us help you."

"If you would help, then leave me in peace," the spirit replied. "Any who come here will be cursed." Her tears had ceased, and anger crept into her voice. River's calming effect was waning.

"You cannot curse me!" Kaiya said boldly, taking a step toward the pool.

"Your magic protects you," the spirit replied coolly. "For now, at least." A wicked laugh escaped her throat.

"We've seen enough," River said to Kaiya. "Keep your focus until we're out of the cave."

Kaiya nodded, knowing that the apparition would attack her if her magic faltered. She followed closely behind River as they made their way through the darkness. Stepping out into the light, both of them dropped their magical defenses.

Lenora rushed to River. "Are you all right?"

"We're fine," he replied. "I know what I'm dealing with now. She is an ancient spirit, and she is capable of great evil. We won't easily be rid of her."

Chapter 22

Pounding on the door of Yiranor's tower with his fist, Telorithan waited impatiently for a servant to answer. When a timid young apprentice finally opened the door, Telorithan shoved him out of the way and entered the tower. He did not spare so much as a glance at the apprentice, who quickly ran up the stairs to fetch his master.

Yiranor hurried down the winding staircase to meet his former student. His hair was in slight disarray, but his face was shining. "Telorithan," he said. "It's nice to have you back so soon."

Telorithan folded his arms. "I've located an elemental." He was in no mood for pointless banter. He already felt delayed by his own misgivings, and he was anxious to get some answers.

169

Yiranor asked, "The Red Isle?"

"No," he replied. "A water elemental who is also an elf."

"Extraordinary!" Yiranor exclaimed. He had never heard of such a thing and was honestly intrigued. "Please, sit. You must tell me everything."

The two elves took seats in the waiting area. Yiranor motioned a servant to bring wine. This could be a lengthy discussion.

"It seems there is an elf living in the Westerling Vale who embodies the spirit of an elemental. I'm not sure how this occurred or who is in control of this body, but he has left the safety of the Vale to visit a dwarf village in the mountains."

"What is he doing there?" Yiranor was puzzled. No elf spent time among the dwarves. They were a boorish race, unworthy of an elf's attention.

"I know not," Telorithan replied with a sigh. "I sense great power in him, and he is not alone."

"A second elemental?" Yiranor's eyes were wide. Was Telorithan considering taking on two of these creatures at once?

"I sense its power, but I can't see it. All I see are dwarves and the two elves who traveled with the elemental."

"Perhaps one of those elves is also an elemental?"

"I don't believe so. I can sense their power, and it is quite weak. One of them is so weak I can barely sense anything from him."

"Do you suppose it could be a dwarf?" Yiranor liked to consider all options, while his former pupil preferred to ignore answers he did not like.

"Have you lost the small amount of mind you have left? How could it possibly be a dwarf?" Redness crept into his face, displaying his anger to his mentor.

"Perhaps one of them is possessed by a spirit just as the elf is."

Silence followed. Telorithan had not considered that scenario. Their nature not being fully understood, elementals were capable of incredible feats of magic. "My question to you is, do you think being half-elf and half-elemental would make this creature more or less powerful? Why would an elemental need an elf body unless it augmented its own power?"

"I cannot say," the old elf replied. "I do know one thing: only the gods possess more power than elementals."

"You mean that an elf body would suppress an elemental's powers." Telorithan spoke more to himself than to Yiranor. Perhaps it was taking elf form merely out of curiosity. Old tales spoke of elementals who grew bored and found strange ways of amusing themselves.

"I don't believe having an elf body would make it more powerful." Yiranor's words were sincere. He doubted Telorithan could tackle a true elemental, but he may well succeed in binding this half-breed. "Unless," he said, thinking out loud, "the elemental were to release itself from the body of the elf, it might no longer be inhibited."

Telorithan's eyes flashed red, his gaze piercing. "I hadn't considered that," he said, sounding uncertain. "Yiranor," he pleaded. "You must help me. I have to find a way to bind an elemental. It's my only hope of binding a god."

Yiranor felt a chill at those words. Before him was an elf obsessed with power, not the young man he had nurtured. The fire in his eyes burned not only with magic, but also with desire. His mind was bent on a single goal, and he needed Yiranor's help. "How could I refuse you?" he replied. "Follow me."

He led his guest up the winding staircase to a room Telorithan had never seen. It was filled with rows of cabinets and wooden boxes of various sizes, all of them labeled with glowing runes. With a quiet giggle,

Yiranor opened a small metal box, and a soft-blue glow illuminated his face. Peering inside, Telorithan beheld a large sapphire. Yiranor reached in and scooped the gem into his hand.

"I enchanted this myself centuries ago," he said proudly. He turned the gem over in his hand, admiring it. "It is flawless and perfectly suited to your needs. You won't find many sapphires of this quality." He placed the gem in Telorithan's hand. "This could soon hold the power of an elemental."

Staring at the gem in his hand, Telorithan was enthralled. "This gem is capable of binding an essence?"

"It is," Yiranor replied. "I know you've only worked with amethysts for soul binding, but an amethyst cannot contain an elemental. Ordinary elves and beasts can be contained in them, but for an elemental, you need higher-quality gems that match your target."

"A sapphire for water," he said, holding the gem up to the light. "Of course. It's so simple I hadn't thought of it."

Yiranor smirked. "I'm happy to be of assistance."

Carefully wrapping the sapphire in a cloth, Telorithan placed it in his pocket. "You have given me a great gift once more. When I have achieved my ultimate goal, your help will not be forgotten."

"I wish you great success," Yiranor replied. He no longer feared what Telorithan might become. Instead, he felt pride. An elf who had grown under his tutelage may someday possess the powers of a god. Perhaps he would bestow a reward upon the elf who had helped him along the way. If he were younger, Yiranor would love to accompany him on this mission. Though he would not be there to witness the event, he knew his student would succeed.

Chapter 23

"Let me at that witch!" Rudi shouted as he burst through a crowd of dwarves. His skin was flushed, and he was sweating. "I'll make her take this curse off, or I'll kill her with my bare hands!" he shouted. "She's the only dwarf to go in that cave and come out healthy. That proves she's the cause!" Immediately after uttering the words, he fell into a coughing fit. Doubling over and clutching his midsection, he continued to cough until he fell to the ground.

Lenora instinctively rushed to his side. None of the dwarves dared to move. She lifted his head from the ground, and he looked up into her pale eyes. Seeing only kindness, Rudi was nearly overcome with emotion. His anger vanished, and his coughing subsided.

"I will take you into the hospital," Lenora said, helping him to his feet.

Rudi followed as if in a trance, entering the tent beside Lenora. She led him to an empty cot where he could rest. After removing his shoes, she brought a bowl of cool water and gently wiped the sweat from his face.

"You're going to be all right," she said, placing a cool cloth on his forehead. "You mustn't believe that Kaiya has caused this. She is only trying to help."

He nodded, unable to argue with the lovely elf maiden. Stirring a small amount of crushed herbs into a glass of water, Lenora pressed the cup to his lips. Within seconds, Rudi was asleep. Repeating the same procedure for the other ailing dwarves, Lenora ensured they would all rest comfortably. She could not break the magic that was causing their pain, but she could minimize their suffering.

She stepped out of the tent to speak with Kaiya. "You mustn't pay heed to his accusations," she said. "He's delirious."

"He's always thought of me as a witch," Kaiya replied with a shrug. "I doubt he will ever see me differently."

Lenora did not reply, but the sadness in her eyes said more than words could express. Her heart was heavy for Kaiya, as well as the suffering dwarves. In her heart, Lenora knew that Kaiya would do anything to save her people. It pained her that the young woman was treated so badly.

"Can you cure this illness?" Galen asked.

Lenora shook her head. "I don't have the skill to break the enchantment. All I can do is try to make them comfortable."

"They must stop drinking water from inside the cave," River said.

"Not only miners are affected," Lenora replied. "Some of the afflicted dwarves are wives and children to the miners. They've never been inside the cave themselves."

"Then it's contagious," Galen remarked, his eyes darting back and forth. "Do you think we can catch it?"

"I don't know," Lenora replied.

"We will find a cure," River declared. "I believe I know who this spirit is." He turned to Galen, "Do you remember tales of Nicodun?"

"Yes," Galen said, nodding. "I read about him while I was working in the archives. He was one of the

First Ones who lived in ancient times. His desire for power led him to commit acts of great evil. When his lover refused to assist him, he murdered her and bound her essence."

"What happened to him?" Kaiya asked.

"He was banished by his kinsmen after he tried to force the Island Dwellers into servitude," Galen replied.

"I believe the apparition inside is that of his lover Indal," River said. "She was murdered here and bound to this place. The dwarves awakened her, and she has nothing left but hatred."

"I think I'd be angry too," Kaiya replied, looking at the cave. "How long has she been trapped?"

"If it's Indal, it's been several millennia since her death," Galen said quietly.

The group remained silent for a moment, absorbing the tragedy of the situation. Indal's anger was understandable, but she was punishing the wrong people. Someone had to stop her before the dwarves were wiped out.

"I will consult with the Spirit of the river in the morning," River said.

"You're leaving?" Lenora asked, surprised.

"No," he replied. "This is the same water that flows into the Vale. I can communicate from here."

"Do you think he knows how to help Indal?" Lenora wished medicine could cure a heart that was broken so long ago, but she knew any effort she made would fail. This was far beyond her skill.

"If there's a way to help her, I believe the Spirit will know," he replied.

"There is one thing I forgot to mention," Galen cut in.

The others turned to look at him, wondering what he had left out.

"Nicodun was banished by the others using an ancient artifact. They required an enchanted opal to destroy him, and they may have destroyed it when they finished with him. There is no record of how it was made or what became of it. It might not be possible to make such an item again."

"My people have great skill with gems and metals. Maybe Trin could craft whatever it is you need." Kaiya sounded hopeful. She had no idea of the power of the First Ones.

"I'm afraid the knowledge of such crafts has long since disappeared," River said. "It's doubtful that anyone could create it."

179

"Then we'll have to find the original," Kaiya declared.

Galen looked doubtful. "There may be nothing to find."

Frustrated, Kaiya replied, "We have to try! We can't stand around talking about how it's hopeless. We have to do something!"

"We will," River promised. "The Spirit will know what to do."

Kaiya sighed. She watched as more dwarves made their way into the hospital tent, some of them barely able to walk. More of her kinsmen were falling ill, and she was powerless to stop it. Ancient magic or not, she wished she had the power to banish the entity herself. She felt sorry for Indal, but she was not justified in her vengeance on the dwarves. There was no excuse for her behavior, and Kaiya would use any means necessary to stop her.

Lenora knelt to embrace Kaiya, who was on the verge of tears. "I will do everything I can for them," she said. "I know you feel it's your duty to save them, and I believe you will do just that. Don't lose heart, my friend. You haven't been defeated yet."

Kaiya watched Lenora as she headed into the tent to treat the new arrivals. Waiting until morning may as well be a month. She was ready to act now, but she had no idea what to do. All she could do was hope that this Spirit would have an answer that would save her people.

Chapter 24

Evening descended over the mountains bringing a deep purple hue to the sky. Lenora had her hands full tending to sick dwarves, whose numbers continued to grow. Bron, the surgeon, had little skill with palliative care. His skills consisted mostly of amputating damaged limbs and administering alcohol to numb pain.

"You're wasting your time with those herbs, Miss Elf," he said quietly to Lenora. His dark eyes showed great sadness, and he was clearly exhausted. "There's no hope for these poor souls."

"We have to keep trying," she responded. "Perhaps you should get some rest. You have grown weary, and I can handle things while you sleep."

Trying to rub the heaviness from his eyelids, he said, "We've lost a patient." Tossing his head, he motioned to the covered form of a dwarf lying on a cot.

Lenora's heart sank seeing that the illness had claimed a second victim. She felt sorry for Indal's plight, but taking the lives of these dwarves was unjustified. "River will be able to stop her," she said. "I'm sure of it."

"Let's hope so," Bron replied, his voice sounding less than hopeful. "I think I will take a rest now. Wake me when you're ready for a break." He headed over to an empty cot and immediately fell asleep.

Outside the tent, Anid and Gerry introduced themselves to River. The town council had taken a great interest in the elven visitors. A few considered them to be a nuisance, but most believed they had come with genuinely good intentions.

"I've heard good things about the lady elf that accompanied you," Anid said. "She's been quite a welcome presence in our hospital."

"She is a skilled healer and will do what she can to comfort the ill," River replied.

"Do you have any idea how to be rid of this evil spirit?" Gerry asked. "Will killing her end the curse?"

"I have no intention of killing her," he replied, ruffling his brow. "She is no longer among the living as it is. My goal is to set her free, allowing her to cross over."

"She deserves to be punished for what she's done to us," Gerry said, feeling no sympathy for Indal.

"For centuries she has lived in torment," River explained. "Her energy is bound to this place. She is trapped, and she is angry."

"That may be true, but she is killing our people. I think we should use any means necessary to be rid of her. I don't care if she suffers further torment."

"You may find compassion can overcome more obstacles than vengeance." River's words were sincere. He would not willingly inflict any more pain on Indal. The agony she had experienced over the years was far more than she deserved. His heart ached for the dwarves who were suffering and dying, but he would not add more suffering to this unfortunate affair.

"If we can set her free, that's what we will do," Kaiya declared. She did not agree with Gerry, and she hoped the situation could be resolved peacefully. Having sensed the spirit's agony firsthand, she had no desire to cause her more harm. There had to be a way to remedy the situation, and Kaiya was determined to see it through, no matter the personal cost.

"Your party should join us for dinner tonight," Anid said, attempting to lighten the mood. "It will be a good distraction for everyone."

Kaiya looked at the ground, knowing that his invitation did not apply to her. Many dwarves would be present at the council house, and she would not be welcome among them. Too many of them still blamed her for the illness, and those who didn't were still suspicious of her magic.

"You may attend as well," Gerry said, noticing Kaiya's withdrawn expression.

She looked up at him in surprise. "Very well," she responded, her voice cracking slightly.

"We'd be delighted," River said. He smiled warmly at Kaiya. "Let's see if we can drag Galen away from Trin long enough to have something to eat."

A few hours later, the elves sat down to dinner with Kaiya and the town council. Fourteen men made up the town's governing body, most of them being of advanced age. The only women present besides Lenora and Kaiya were cooks and servers.

"Why are there no women among your government?" Lenora asked.

"Women are expected to marry and raise children," Kaiya replied. "Then we help our husbands with their businesses and tend to our homes. That's how it is, and no one ever steps up to change it."

"Maybe someone should," Lenora said, narrowing her eyes.

Kaiya glanced around at the councilmen. Lenora had not been quiet when speaking, and many of them had obviously heard her words. They looked uneasy, but did not express their opinions.

Galen sipped at the frothy brown ale in the large mug before him. "This is excellent," he declared, wiping his mouth with his sleeve.

Kaiya enjoyed the ale as well, and even River partook of the stout beverage. Only Lenora declined the drink, fearing it may dull her senses. She would need all of them to tend her patients the next day.

The councilmen raised their mugs and pounded their fists on the table as they lifted their voices in song. Conversation was kept light to distract the dinner guests from the plague affecting the town. They talked of the fine weather and how the elves had traveled into the mountains. Little was said of the evil presence lurking within the cave. Fear and worry were thrown aside briefly, allowing the dwarves to put their minds at ease.

* * * * *

Ryllak paced on the bank of the river near the waterfall, wondering if his son had found the dwarf village. Had River and his companions fallen ill as well? Had he faced the evil presence in the mountains? Ryllak could not stop his mind from worrying.

He waded into the water, hoping the Spirit could hear him. "Spirit," he said. "I worry for my son's safety. Can you take me to him?"

The roar of the waterfall was the only sound to be heard as Ryllak stood waist-deep in the water, hoping for a reply. Then, the water fell silent. To his surprise, the waterfall had ceased to flow. The staircase leading into the mountains had reappeared, presenting itself beneath the moonlight.

Looking into the water, Ryllak said, "Thank you, Spirit." He hurried to the staircase and began to climb, his heart anxious to find his son. He climbed into the darkness, fearing not the night.

Chapter 25

River awoke before dawn, anxious to converse with

the Spirit. He walked softly to avoid waking his
companions as he exited the council house. A few
miles north of the town was one of the streams that
flowed into the Blue River below. It was summer in
the mountains, and the water would be flowing
quickly. River could sense its presence and found it
easily, despite the darkness of the sky.

Stepping into the cold waters, River felt no chill. He
was part of this stream, and he was at home here.
Immersing himself to his waist, he cupped his hands
to scoop the water and pour it over his head. A pale-
orange light filled the sky as the sun awoke, ready to
begin a new day. The Spirit came to River, its presence
filling the water as the sun filled the sky.

River's hope that the Spirit could provide the answers he sought was not in vain. The Spirit had existed for years beyond count, and knew of Nicodun and Indal. The artifact needed to free Indal from her binding had not been destroyed. It had been placed deep in the ocean where it could not be used for ill purpose. No elf, human, or dwarf could hope to reach it at its depths. Only a creature of the water could hope to retrieve it. Though saddened by this revelation, River knew he would have to journey alone.

Slowly emerging from the water, River noticed a figure in the distance and knew instantly who had arrived. He lifted a hand in greeting to his father. "What brings you here?" he asked. "Is there trouble in the Vale?"

Ryllak shook his head. "No, nothing like that. I worried for you, that's all."

River seemed unbothered by his father's sudden appearance. Though he was grown, he still appreciated his father's concern. "I'm quite well, Father."

"I see that," Ryllak replied, feeling slightly embarrassed. "I suppose you didn't need me, but I worried you may have fallen ill." He wrung his hands, unsure of what to say next. It was difficult to accept that his son did not need his help anymore.

Sensing his father's discomfort, River said, "I will always look for your guidance, Father."

Ryllak patted his son on the back. "You must never be afraid to ask for it," he said. "I know you have a great destiny ahead of you, but you must never be too proud to ask for help. If I have taught you anything, I hope I have taught you that you do have friends, and they are most willing to help you." Finishing his speech, Ryllak felt a weight lifted from his shoulders. "As a father, it's difficult to know you've given a child enough knowledge to go off into the world." He laughed softly and shook his head.

"You've given me much over the years, Father," River replied. "I am grateful to you."

Ryllak smiled, and the two proceeded into the dwarven village. Quite a few citizens were already preparing for the day despite the early hour. The marketplace stalls were being stocked, and fresh baked goods were coming out of the oven, filling the air with an appetizing aroma.

"Oh great, another elf!" a dwarf exclaimed as the pair walked by. "We'll be overrun soon!"

His words generated a bit of interest in the new arrival, but the general sentiment was calm. Father and son took seats near the council house.

"I have discovered what is causing the illness," River said. "An ancient elf was murdered here. Her spirit was bound by her lover, and she has dwelt here for many centuries. The miners disturbed her rest, and she awoke with a vengeance."

"Do you know how to stop her?" Ryllak asked.

"There is an ancient artifact, an opal, that I must retrieve. It lies at the bottom of the ocean near the Sunswept Isles."

Ryllak was too stunned to reply at first. After a moment, he asked, "How will you retrieve it?"

"Swim," River replied with a shrug.

Ryllak took a deep breath. "You can make it safely to those depths?"

"Of course I can," he replied. "The Spirit has said so."

"The Spirit may have this capability, but you have the body of an elf. We are not indestructible."

"All will be well, Father," River said reassuringly.

Galen emerged from a stall behind the smithy and was surprised to see Ryllak had come. He approached the pair with a wide smile on his face. "Good morning," he said. "Any news?"

"I thought you were still sleeping," River replied.

"I woke early and saw that you were gone. I decided to help Trin set up for the day's work. Rune carving is truly quite fascinating."

"Sounds like you've finally found something interesting to study," Ryllak commented.

Galen shrugged. "It's certainly not something I can learn in the Vale."

"What of Lenora and Kaiya? Are they still inside?" River asked.

"They were when I left," he replied. Stepping onto the porch, Galen peeked inside the council house. There was no one to be seen. "I guess they got up early too."

"Lenora will be with her patients," River said. He had no doubt as to where she would be. Her dedication to the ailing dwarves was absolute. River admired her compassion and desire to help the sick.

"Kaiya could be anywhere," Galen remarked. "She probably went back into that cave."

River looked concerned. "I hope not." Kaiya had been unsettled by their last encounter with the entity, and she was impatient to find a solution. Her magic was strong, but she could not expel the presence alone. Without the opal, neither of them could hope to accomplish such a task.

"We'll have to find her. I want to tell her what I've learned, and then I need to be on my way."

"Wait, you're leaving?" Galen said, shock registering in his voice.

"I have to retrieve the artifact to free Indal. It's the only way to end the plague."

"I'm going with you," Galen said firmly.

"You can't," River replied. "I'm going to the bottom of the ocean. You won't make it, I'm afraid."

"I don't care," he replied, shaking his head. "I will wait on the shore. You're not going by yourself."

Glancing back at his father, River's mouth opened to speak, but no words came out. Ryllak smiled slightly and lifted his eyebrows. Though Galen had difficulty finding focus in his life, he was a true friend to River. He may have been a troublemaker in his youth, but Ryllak knew he would stand at River's side through good or bad. There was no better person to accompany his son, and he was happy to hear Galen so determined to travel with him.

"Don't bother arguing," Galen said. "I'll only follow if you try to leave without me."

"I will be pleased to have your company," River admitted. "We should let Lenora and Kaiya know before we leave."

Rising to his feet, Ryllak said, "I'll be waiting for you in the Vale, my son. Safe journeys to both of you." He hugged River tightly before turning to leave. Though he still felt some worry, his mind was more at ease. River seemed confident in his abilities, and Ryllak did not doubt him. Hopefully, he would be seeing his son again soon.

Chapter 26

Sitting quietly behind a tree, Kaiya focused her mind on the wind. The breeze was light that morning, but its voice was strong. Tiny sparks danced on her fingertips as the wind gently caressed her hands. *Tell me how to release Indal.* She projected her thoughts to the wind, hoping for an answer. The voice on the wind seemed to reply, but she could not make out the words.

"I don't understand," she said to herself in frustration. Placing her head in her hands, she sighed. The wind tousled her hair, tickling the sides of her face.

From behind, she heard a mournful cry pierce the air. Hopping to her feet, she turned quickly to see a dwarf woman and child standing outside the hospital tent. They were clutching each other tightly and sobbing. *Another life has been lost,* she thought. She closed her eyes and felt her heart grow heavy. *This has to stop. Whatever it takes, this must end.*

Hoping that River had learned how to free Indal, Kaiya set out to find him. Her mind was made up. No more families should have to mourn a loss. If Indal could not be freed peacefully, she would have to be forced out. Kaiya felt sorry for Indal's suffering, but if she refused to relent, Kaiya would use any means necessary to be rid of her. She might not succeed in an attack on Indal, but she would gladly give her life in the attempt.

Near the council house, Kaiya spotted River and Galen. A third elf appeared to be walking away. Wondering who he might be, she quickened her pace until she reached the pair.

"Who was that?" she asked, pointing at Ryllak.

"My father," River replied. "He was worried and wanted to give me some advice."

"Did you speak with your Spirit?" she asked.

"I did," he replied. "I must travel to the coast and enter the sea. The artifact we need is there."

"And you're sure this will be the end of it? No more dwarves will die once you have this artifact?"

"I am certain," he replied.

"Good. I'll come with you." She straightened her back to stand as tall as she could. This mission was as important to her as any other, and she would not be held back from it.

Galen grinned at River. "Looks like it's a party."

"Of course you can come," River replied.

"I didn't ask permission," she said casually. "This is my fight, and I will see it to its end. If your plan fails, I will find another way, no matter the cost."

"Let us hope the plan succeeds," River said. "There is no need to bring harm to Indal. This opal can free her from her suffering. After that, she will have no more cause to harm your people."

"She has no cause to harm them now," Kaiya argued. "She must be stopped, peacefully or not." Her words were true. She would go to any length to prevent another dwarf's death. She could not bear the sight of another devastated family.

"Let's hope River's plan works," Galen commented. "Indal may prove much harder to destroy if it doesn't."

"She is an ancient," River replied. "If this opal doesn't work, there might not be a way to stop her. All we can do is hope."

199

Kaiya knew his words made sense, but she was tired of hoping. Now was the time for action. "Let's be on our way," she said.

"I need to tell Lenora we are leaving," River said.

The trio headed to the medical tent where Lenora was busy with patients. More had arrived seeking care. Dozens of cots were now occupied, and there was little room for more. Kaiya bowed her head, wishing she had the power to heal these dwarves.

Lenora gave a weak smile and tried to smooth her disheveled hair as River approached. "You bring news?" she asked.

"We are leaving for the coast to retrieve an artifact," he explained. "I hope it will result in the end of this illness."

"I wish you success," she said. "I'll be here tending to these dwarves until you return."

Boldly, River leaned in and kissed her lips. She was surprised, but the kiss was not unwelcome.

"I will see you again soon," he said, his eyes shining brightly.

Lenora nodded. To Kaiya, she said, "Take care of these guys for me."

"I will," she responded.

The three of them exited the tent without looking back. Their mission was clear, and it was time they set out.

"We can stop by my parents' farm on the way. They have food we can take, and I know of a path that will lead us to the coast. If we move quickly, we can be there in two days' time."

"Lead the way," Galen replied cheerfully.

They followed Kaiya down the rocky path between the village and her home. The countryside gave way to green pastures nestled under the shadow of the mountains. Doozle greeted the party as they approached the farmhouse. He stretched playfully with his head low to the ground, his wagging tail high in the air.

Darvil took notice of their approach and looked at the elves with distrust.

"These elves are our friends, Papa," Kaiya said, reading his expression. "They've come to help us cure the sickness."

Darvil looked confused. "Elves?"

River stepped forward to shake Darvil's hand. "Greetings," he said. "You have an exceptionally talented daughter."

Kaiya blushed despite herself. "This is River," she said. "And this is Galen."

"Pleased to meet you," Darvil grumbled, still unsure what to make of the visitors.

"I'm taking them to the coast to retrieve an item that will help. We need some supplies." Kaiya headed inside where her mother was knitting.

"Kaiya," she said, standing. "You were gone all night."

"I made some new friends," she replied. "We had dinner at the council house and spent the night there."

Kassie peered curiously out the window at her husband and the two elves. "Those are interesting friends," she commented.

"I'm showing them the way to the coast. We need some food and blankets to take with us."

Pulling herself away from the window, Kassie said, "Of course." She hurried into the kitchen to collect some food items from the pantry.

Kaiya grabbed three blankets from her room and rolled them into bundles. Kassie handed her a shoulder bag full of dried meat, nuts, and fruit.

"I'm not sure what elves eat," Kassie remarked. Grabbing a fresh loaf of bread from the table, she added it to Kaiya's bag.

"Thanks, Mum," she said before hugging her mother.

"You be careful," Kassie replied. "Don't be afraid to use your magic if you need it."

With a nod, Kaiya stepped outside to rejoin her friends. She was surprised to hear laughter between her father and the elves. Darvil was not the sort of man to trust quickly, but it seemed he was charmed by River and Galen. No doubt River's ability to bring calm to a situation had helped.

"I think I have everything," Kaiya said.

"Take care of my little girl," Darvil said to the elves. "She can be a handful, but she's a good daughter." He chuckled quietly, his eyes gleaming.

"I will keep both eyes on her, even if I trip over a rock because of it," Galen pledged, placing a hand over his heart.

"She will be quite safe," River promised. Believing the journey would be uneventful, River made this promise easily.

With Kaiya leading the way, the trio turned away from the road and crossed the green pasture. The path to the coast was rarely used, and few dwarves had knowledge of it. Though Kaiya had not made the journey since she was a child, she remembered the way. With the wind as her guide, she could see the path that had formerly been cut through the short mountain grass, but she failed to notice the eyes that were watching her from a distance.

Chapter 27

After leaving Yiranor's tower, Telorithan decided to pay Sirra a visit as well. Her presence was not wholly intolerable, and she had her moments of brilliance. If she couldn't provide real assistance, she could at least be useful in spreading the news of his success. He did not personally wish to be bothered with questions, so she would be the perfect person to carry the news of his triumph to the world. Once he managed to bind a god, he would no longer need any other elf. Until the process was perfected, however, he would be wise to seek counsel from other accomplished sorcerers.

Letting himself into her tower without knocking, he surprised a female servant with his presence.

"Tell your mistress I am here," he said.

The elf curtsied before running up the stairs to find Sirra.

"Telorithan?" Sirra said, coming down the stairs. "I am surprised to see you."

"I was unkind to you during our last visit," he admitted. He spoke matter-of-factly, his voice showing no hint of regret.

"Yes, you were," she replied, crossing her arms. "I suppose you have been under stress. I'm glad you have come." She managed a smile and came to his side at the bottom of the stairs.

Pulling the large sapphire from his pocket, he presented it to Sirra. "Yiranor has graced me with this gorgeous gem," he said, pride filling his voice. "With this I will bind the water elemental."

"The elemental you had no knowledge of until I told you about him," Sirra remarked. Her voice was smug. Telorithan was not quick to show his gratitude, and she yearned for him to appreciate her. Her physical attraction to him could not be denied, and she knew he was attracted to her as well. Getting him to show it was not always easy.

"You did indeed," he admitted. "Without you, I might still be searching." He reached for her hand and pressed it against his lips. His blue eyes locked on hers, and she blushed at his unusually tender gesture.

"You are a unique elf," she said, allowing herself to relax. "Why have you come?"

"Why, to see you of course." A mischievous grin appeared on his lips. Flattery usually worked easily on Sirra. She was a beautiful woman who loved to capture a man's attention. Telorithan knew how strongly she felt for him, and he was willing to take advantage of that.

She gave him a sly look as she attempted to read his true motives. "I know better," she said. "You have never been one to make a social call. Tell me what you need of me."

"I need your mind, Sirra," he said, walking away. He took a seat on one of her opulent chairs, tossing a velvet cushion to the floor. Sirra had a flare for decorating, and her tower was filled with too many pillows on too many pieces of furniture.

Taking a seat next to him and pressing her body into his, she said, "I'd love to help you." Her words were quiet, almost whispered into his ear. She could feel his anxiety, his normal cocky air being strangely absent. Perhaps he wasn't as perfect as he tried to present himself. He was doubting his abilities and had come to her for reassurance.

"I need practice," he admitted. "I've bound only one elf, and elementals are quite powerful." He looked at the floor as if speaking to himself. "I cannot fail. I might not get a second chance."

Sirra ran her fingers over his silver hair and nestled her face into the curve of his neck. He closed his eyes, enjoying her warmth. Her presence was comforting to his troubled mind. Though he normally preferred solitude, Sirra had a way of endearing herself to him at times. Today, he was glad to have her at his side.

An idea came to Sirra's mind. "You could challenge another master to a duel," she suggested. "If you win, you can bind his essence."

Slightly offended, he replied, "*If* I win? You mean *when.*"

"Of course," she said, not wanting to argue.

"The practice is banned. Have you forgotten?" He shook his head at her foolishness. "If I am seen binding the essence of anyone, I'll be exiled. The entire crowd could turn on me. Even I couldn't defend against hundreds of attackers."

"I've never seen the process," she replied. "Neither has any other elf on these islands. How are you so sure they'll know what you're doing?"

"It isn't a pretty process," he said, remembering the agony of the thief. "The crowd will catch on quickly when they see it."

Sirra thought for a moment. "I guess there's only one other way, then."

Telorithan stared at her, waiting for her to finish her thought.

"You'll have to murder someone." She spoke casually as if it was nothing. "You've taken lives before, so do it again."

Telorithan briefly remembered the faces of the bandits who attacked his classmates many years ago. He had made short work of killing them. His anger had not ended there, and others were caught in his wrath. This time was different. He would have time to plan rather than acting on instinct. With the essence of another master at his command, he should have enough power to best the elemental in battle. Sirra's idea was brilliant.

"I would be delighted to assist you," she said, her fingers caressing his face. "We'll find someone elderly who won't put up too much of a fight."

His eyes narrowed as his anger rose. "You think me incapable of besting a sorcerer with full strength?"

"Not at all," she said softly. "You showed me that the elemental is on the move. You might have to leave at a moment's notice, and you don't want your power to be drained when you meet him. Let me do most of the work, and you can handle the binding."

Sirra's calculating mind impressed him. He had not considered his own power stores. It was true that the elemental was on the move, and he had no idea when they would eventually come to blows. "I accept your offer," he said.

"Good," she replied. "Now all that remains is to decide who is dead."

Chapter 28

After a long day's walk, the group decided to make camp for the night. The sun was setting fast behind the mountains, and the air was growing cooler. They had reached the sparse evergreen forest that sat above the base of the mountain. There was only a small amount of fallen wood available for a fire.

"I can create sparks from the air to make fire, but I'm afraid there isn't enough wood here," Kaiya explained. "I think it's going to be a cold night." She looked up at the pale, glowing moon.

"There are plenty of rocks," Galen said with a shrug. "We'll use those."

Placing what little wood she could find within a circle of rocks, Kaiya closed her eyes and focused on the wind. As the sparks appeared at her fingertips, she flung them onto the wood. A small fire was born, crackling itself to life.

"I'm afraid it won't last long," she said.

River knelt at her side and placed his hands upon the rocks surrounding the fire. Blue magic emitted from his hands, giving the rocks a soft sapphire glow. As Kaiya sat intrigued, the magic spread over the wood, changing the orange fire to blue.

"It will last all night," River said with a smile.

Kaiya held her hands near the fire to warm them. To her surprise, her entire body felt warmed, not just her hands. Though the fire was quite small, it produced heat to rival a campfire five times its size.

"You'll have to teach me that one," she said, laughing.

"He has lots of tricks," Galen said, taking a seat next to her. "This particular one is nothing more than elf magic, though."

"So I can't learn it since I'm a dwarf?" Kaiya took the comment as a challenge. She had always made an effort to do what people said she couldn't.

"Kaiya can pull the warmth from the air to create fire," River commented. "She simply hasn't tried yet."

He was right. Kaiya hadn't journeyed away from home without her father before. He knew how to build a fire, and he always traveled prepared. She had never had the need for such magic. The idea of pulling the wind's energy to create fire hadn't occurred to her.

"If you haven't seen me do it, how do you know I can?" She wondered how he could be so knowledgeable about her abilities. They hadn't known each other long, yet he seemed to understand her magic perhaps better than she understood it herself. "Maybe you can also tell me why I can do magic when no other dwarf seems capable of the simplest spells."

"You are more special than you realize, Kaiya," River said.

"I've never had any training," she admitted. "I listen to the wind, and the magic comes to me." She had never understood the process, but she had accepted it gladly. Even small feats of magic could lift her spirits when she was sad. There was something about magic that could always cheer her, as if it were a friend to keep her company.

"You will have many long years to learn," he replied.

"Maybe for a dwarf," she said. "Elves have many more years to learn than we do."

"Your life will extend far beyond that of an average dwarf. I can see it."

Kaiya looked up at him, her eyes widening. "What do you mean?"

"Your magic grants you the lifespan of the First Ones," he explained. "You will have to decide when you are ready to cross over."

"The First Ones?" she asked.

"My kind."

"So I'll outlive everyone I care about," she said with sorrow. She thought of her mother and father and even her dog Doozle. It was expected that she would outlive all of them, but she hadn't considered what it would be like to be alone. How many generations would she see come and go? "How long do your kind live?"

"It depends," he replied. "Most of us cross over after about five thousand years. Some feel the urge to leave sooner, and others have stayed longer." He turned to face her. "It's a choice, Kaiya."

She swallowed, feeling a lump in her throat. Staring into the fire, she asked, "Can you really see my future?"

"Some of it, yes," he admitted.

"I don't have the gift of foresight," she said with regret. "I might have prevented the plague before it began if I had such a gift."

"I doubt you could have prevented anything," he said. "The gift of foresight is new to me. I fear what I might see in times to come." It was certain that he would see many unpleasant things to come in the world of Nōl'Deron, and he did not look forward to those events. Since coming of age, he had seen only a few events. All of them had been pleasant. In time, however, he would begin to see things he did not wish to see. He feared that someday he might see the loss of friends or the destruction of the Vale. He placed those worries far from his mind, knowing it would do no good to fear such things now. Whatever was yet to come, he would deal with it as it showed itself.

"I'm not sure I like the idea of deciding when to end my own life," Kaiya said. *How do people choose when they're ready for their life to be over?* Looking to her left, she noticed that Galen had wrapped himself in his blanket and had fallen asleep next to the fire. *That's why he's been so quiet,* she thought, chuckling silently to herself. She pulled her blanket around her shoulders to block out the cool night air.

"You should visit the Vale someday," River said. "Perhaps one of the elders can assist you with your magic."

"I think I'd like that," she replied. The elves could probably teach her many other things in addition to magic. In her mind, she pictured the Vale as a land of enchantment. She wondered if the wind spoke louder there. After yawning twice, she said, "I guess we should try to get some sleep." She curled up next to the fire, falling asleep within seconds.

River sat silently by the fire as darkness crept through the mountains, enveloping the world in night. From the flames, he sensed the presence of magic. Watchful eyes were observing him, their intentions unclear. They were unfamiliar to him, not the eyes of a worried father. Somewhere, a magical being was keeping track of him. Even the darkness could not shield him from its gaze.

Chapter 29

Racing up the twisted staircase with Sirra a few steps behind, Telorithan felt exhilarated. He entered the laboratory and chose a sparkling amethyst gemstone to hold the essence of his victim. The pair had decided on an elderly elf by the name of Master Koru. At nearly twenty-eight hundred years of age, he was already past the life expectancy of most Enlightened Elves. In his prime, he had wielded great power. In death, he would share that power with Telorithan.

Koru's tower was less than a mile from Telorithan's home. It was likely no one would notice him during the short journey. Having been present at an inquest against Telorithan some centuries ago, Koru had voted in favor of his imprisonment. With such a motive in place, Telorithan was determined to make his death appear natural, thus avoiding suspicion.

Sirra had agreed to assist, even if that meant dealing the deathblow herself. Her level of excitement was high, and her eyes gleamed with anticipation. She wondered how it would feel to hold another elf's essence in her hands. Such thoughts only increased her craving, giving her a wild, savage feeling.

Telorithan remained calm and composed. His heart was racing, but he did not show it outwardly. Though his prey was elderly, he still might fight back. Sirra would have to be prepared to step in to preserve Telorithan's magical supply. He couldn't risk exhaustion. If his magic were depleted, he would have no chance of binding the elemental should he be forced to confront it. He must use as little of his own power as possible.

He passed the gem to Sirra, allowing her to admire it. Pressing it to her lips, she said, "A kiss for luck."

"We won't need luck," he scoffed. "All I need is you to keep your promise."

"Of course I shall," she replied. Giving him a wicked smile, she placed the gem back in his hand. "I am yours," she said seductively.

"There's no point in waiting any longer," he said. "We have what we need."

He took her by the hand as they descended the staircase and exited the tower. There were no other elves to be seen in the streets as they walked toward the elderly master's tower. Sirra would have to gain entry while Telorithan remained unseen. No one would accuse Sirra of murder. She was well liked, even though she had been seen in Telorithan's company on many occasions. No doubt most of her friends felt sorry for her. She was pursuing a man who would never return her affections.

Stepping to the side of the tower, he hid himself from the sight of any servants who would be standing near the entrance. Sirra grasped the large brass ring on the front of the door and struck it once against the wood. A servant answered almost instantly.

"May I help you?" the petite elf asked.

"I've come to pay a visit to Master Koru. Is he in?"

"Yes, Mistress," the girl replied. "May I tell him who is visiting?"

"I am Dahlia," Sirra lied. If this servant did not know her identity, there was no reason to divulge the truth.

"Have a seat in the waiting area," the servant instructed.

Sirra stepped inside, pretending to close the door behind her. The servant disappeared up the stairs, and Sirra quickly turned to motion Telorithan inside. Making sure no one was watching, he glanced to each side before entering the tower. Immediately he hid himself behind the heavy velvet drapes that adorned a large window.

The servant descended the stairs to find Sirra standing casually near the door. "I'm sorry, Mistress," she began. "He doesn't recognize your name. At his age, his memory isn't all that good. I expect he'll recognize your face when he sees you. Fifth floor at the end of the hall." She curtsied and stepped aside to allow Sirra access to the staircase.

"Thank you," Sirra replied, placing a hand on the railing.

Telorithan peeked from the curtains and watched the servant turn away. As she disappeared down a corridor, he tiptoed to the staircase to join Sirra. He was not a fan of sneaking around, but if he were seen on the day of Koru's death, there would certainly be an inquiry into the matter. Koru was a former member of the Grand Council, and he had many friends.

Telorithan, on the other hand, was disliked almost universally. He had escaped punishment for crimes on a few occasions, and many believed him guilty of murder. He was a dangerous elf to be near.

Master Koru sat propped on his bed. He had taken ill a few days earlier, but he seemed to be on the mend. The color had returned to his wrinkled face, and he had managed to eat breakfast that morning. It seemed he was not prepared for the grave just yet.

He eyed Sirra suspiciously as she entered the room. It was obvious he did not know her. When Telorithan stepped in behind her, he was recognized immediately.

"You," Koru said, anger filling his eyes. "What are you doing here?" Their dealings in the past had not been pleasant. Koru had sat on the Grand Council when Telorithan was charged with murdering three classmates. The evidence had been unreliable, and Telorithan was acquitted. Koru, however, believed him to be guilty and lucky to escape justice.

"I've come for a visit, dear friend," Telorithan said mockingly.

Without giving the elderly elf a chance to react, Telorithan extended his hands, shooting an orange beam of light at his victim. The old man was paralyzed instantly, his face twisted in agony.

Telorithan stepped closer, still maintaining the spell. "You wanted to send me into exile all those years ago," he said. "All these years you have hated me. Now you will hate me for eternity." He lifted the gemstone from his pocket and presented it before Koru's eyes.

Koru knew exactly what Telorithan intended. The practice of soul binding was banned, but a criminal would not abide by such laws. Koru had seen the process used in his youth, and he had never forgotten it.

Sirra stepped forward to take over the spell. Dark-green magic replaced the orange as she held Koru in place. Telorithan readied the gem and sent a beam of purple light into the old man's heart. As Koru attempted to struggle, Sirra's magic spread over his face, covering his nose and mouth. The paralysis spell was lifted, allowing her to focus only on suffocating her victim. He kicked wildly as he struggled to find his breath. His green eyes pleaded with the dark-haired woman, vainly hoping she would stop this madness and spare his life.

After a moment, he ceased his struggle, the life draining from his body. Telorithan's eyes stared greedily as the old elf's essence traveled toward the gem he held in his hands. As it found its way inside, the stone vibrated uncontrollably. In an instant, it shattered, cutting deep gashes into his hand. Instinctively, he grabbed it to stop the bleeding, his mind in shock at his failure. Sirra rushed to his side, using her magic to seal the wounds.

"The gem," he said, dumbfounded. He looked at its remains lying on the ground. It was little more than dust. "I've failed," he said quietly. "The gem is destroyed."

Sirra tried to comfort him. "The gem was likely flawed," she suggested.

"No," he replied, his face becoming hot. "This is your fault. You were too long in killing him."

Sirra was stunned by his accusation. "I did everything I could," she said, trying to keep her voice down. The last thing they needed were nosy servants poking their heads in. "We need to get out of here."

With a wave of his hand, Telorithan collected the remains of the amethyst. Sirra took them in her hands and led the way down the staircase. Luckily, the servant had not returned, and the pair left the tower in silence.

The sun was high overhead, but still the streets remained empty. Sirra was grateful for the solitude. Telorithan walked as if in a trance, unable to accept that the procedure had failed. Slowly they approached his tower and stepped inside.

Sirra wrapped her arms around him and said, "We will try again." She tried to sound encouraging. "I'll do whatever it takes to ensure your success next time." In her clenched hand, she still held the remains of the amethyst. She opened her palm to let him inspect them.

Staring at the purple remnants, he said, "You're right. The gem was flawed." He placed a hand against his forehead. "How could I have missed that!" he screamed in frustration. Turning away from Sirra, he picked up a wine bottle and threw it into the fireplace, smashing it to pieces. The light of the flames within caught his eye, and he stared into their hypnotic glow.

Chapter 30

Crushing some herbs between her fingers, Lenora sprinkled them into a glass of warm water. Her supplies were running low as more and more dwarves were coming in for treatment. The illness seemed to be spreading faster, and she had no idea if she could cure it. So far, most of her patients had responded to a mixture of yarrow and cherry bark. Though it was far from being a cure, it did help alleviate a few symptoms.

This morning, she had noticed one elderly dwarf whose situation was critical. Her herbs had done little to soothe his suffering, and she hoped this new mixture would bring him some comfort. Pressing the glass to the ailing man's lips, she hoped that anise and thyme would do the trick. He coughed a bit after drinking, but after a few minutes he relaxed. As she wiped his forehead with a cloth, he looked into her pale eyes.

"I've never seen an elf before," he said. "You are the prettiest thing I've ever seen."

Lenora smiled softly. "Thank you," she said.

The old man took her hand and pressed it to his heart. As his eyes closed, Lenora knew immediately that he was dying. Laying her hand on the side of his face, she said, "Stay with me."

There was no reply. Only the sound of his final breath reached her ears. Tears fell quickly from her eyes as she covered the man's face with a blanket. Losing a patient was part of being a healer at times, but she hoped she would never become accustomed to it. So far, she had lost three dwarves under her care. Each one weighed heavily on her heart, making her more determined to help the rest. She wondered if her friends were having any luck finding the artifact and how long it would be before they returned.

She continued checking on patients, hoping to work through her grief. Bron would handle the grim task of informing the man's family. It was best for them to hear such news from a trusted member of their community. Lenora didn't mind being spared from that burden.

A dwarf woman entered the tent, her expression showing her surprise at the number of patients inside. Lenora couldn't help thinking she bore a striking resemblance to Kaiya. The woman was heavier and had graying hair, but their similarities were too many to be coincidental.

On seeing Lenora, the woman walked carefully between rows of cots to reach her. "I've come to offer my help," she said.

"Are you a nurse?" Lenora asked.

"No," she replied. "My daughter has gone away to find help, and I thought I might be able to help here. I don't have medical training, but I can do whatever you need me to do."

"You're Kaiya's mother, aren't you?" Lenora replied with a tired smile.

"I am," she replied. "My name's Kassie."

"I'm Lenora," she said, extending her hand. "Your help is most welcome. You could grind some of these herbs and administer them to the sick." Gesturing to the vials on the desk, she asked, "Are you familiar with any of these?" She hoped Kassie would know at least a few herbs, saving her the time it would take to explain.

"I know ginger by looks," she said, looking over the vials. "Some of the others I'll recognize by smell." She popped a cork from the top of one vial and lifted it close to her nose. Inhaling deeply, she said, "Yellowroot."

"Good," Lenora replied. "I'm having luck with some combinations. You can grind those first." Grabbing three vials, she placed them in front of Kassie.

"I need two parts of the first vial mixed with one part of each of the others," she explained. "One teaspoon dissolved in warm water seems to help with cough and fever."

Kassie nodded that she understood.

"Nurse!" one of the female patients cried. "Please! Nurse!"

Lenora rushed from her seat to tend to the woman's needs. Kassie ground the herbs in a stone bowl, occasionally glancing over at Lenora. The elf maiden had a gentle quality about her, and it was easy to see that she cared for her patients. After tending the woman, she checked on several other patients before returning to her seat.

"You're more doctor than nurse, I think," Kassie commented.

"A title isn't important," Lenora replied. "I'm a healer. Whatever term a person wants to use for it is fine with me."

"You certainly do a better job than Bron," Kassie said. "Most dwarves never experience care again like they had with their mothers. The men always think they're supposed to be tough, at least in front of other men." She chuckled a bit, knowing how childish her own husband could be when he had a minor scrape or bruise.

"That might change after this experience," Lenora remarked.

"You may be right. Do you have magic that could heal them?"

"I've tried to no avail," she replied. "The curse that is causing this illness is too strong for me to break. I've used magic to help with some symptoms, but there are so many patients that I run out quickly."

"I didn't know magical beings could run out of magic," Kassie commented. "I've never known Kaiya to run out."

"Kaiya is special," Lenora said. "I'm only an elf."

229

Lana Axe

"Yes, Kaiya is very special," she replied proudly. "I think you're pretty special too, though. You have shown these people a level of compassion that certainly isn't common around here." She finished grinding the herbs and placed them in a vial. "All done," she said.

"Thank you," Lenora replied. "You can administer it to some of the patients if you like. Anyone who is still coughing can have another dose. Any patients who are restless may still have fever. They can have more medicine as well."

Kassie nodded and headed to the farthest side of the tent to check on the patients. After raising five children, nursing the sick came easily to her. It was a welcome distraction from worrying about Kaiya. She had no idea where her daughter was going or what she might face when she got there. Perhaps she would return with a cure. Until she made it back safely, Kassie would do her part to help.

Chapter 31

The first stars were appearing in the sky as Telorithan sat in front of the fireplace in his laboratory. Hesitating for a moment, he wondered if he should bother tracking the water elemental. His failure to bind Master Koru had left him shaken. This being was almost certain to be stronger than Koru, even if it was trapped within an elf body. *I must do this,* he thought. *I must have this creature's power.*

Putting his doubts aside, he gazed intently into the flames. The image of two elves and a dwarf appeared before his eyes. They were walking carefully down a rocky slope, laughing and talking as they descended. Telorithan could sense the elemental, and also the weak powers of the second elf. There must have been something unseen traveling with them, however. The magic he had sensed before was still present, and its power was just as strong. *What can it be?*

Being a dwarf, Kaiya possessing magic was unthinkable to him. She could not possibly account for any magical presence, especially one so strong. *What if the dwarf is carrying something?* The thought sent shivers through his body. Dwarves were well known for their ability to delve deep into the earth. Perhaps this one had discovered something and was using it to assist the elemental.

Any object that could enhance the elf's abilities would create unknown complications in Telorithan's plan. Elementals possess intense magical powers, and they do not tire easily. As an elf, Telorithan would have limits that might not apply to his opponent. He hoped being trapped in elf form would inhibit this water elemental. The idea of facing one at full strength might not be possible after his failure to augment his power with Koru's.

The second elf didn't appear to be much of a problem. He would be easily dispatched with a wave of Telorithan's hand. Still, he hoped the other two would not be present when he finally faced his enemy. Expending his magical stores against only the elemental would be ideal. Who knows how much magic would be needed to defeat him? Spending one drop on the second elf or the useless dwarf would be a terrible waste.

He wondered if it would be wise to invite Sirra to fight alongside him. She could handle the other two, allowing him to focus only on the elemental. He still blamed her somewhat for his failure with Master Koru. Had she not distracted him, he would have inspected the gem more thoroughly and noticed the flaw. Her constant flaunting of her sexuality had no doubt been the reason for his negligence. Who could possibly focus on the task at hand with her in the room?

Sirra, he decided, would not be allowed to accompany him. Even if it meant using more magic than he hoped, she would still be a distraction. His failure would be assured with her around, so he made up his mind to travel alone. He regretted using the thief's essence for the fire, even if it had been a necessary sacrifice. Without it, he couldn't have located the elemental. Still, the small amount of power the gem had held could have been useful in his fight.

As he stared unblinking into the flames, he noticed movement in the background. Bits of moonlight reflected in and out of focus in a rhythmic pattern.

They've reached the ocean, he realized. Still unsure of their purpose, he hesitated only a moment. They were traveling away from the rising moon, which meant they were heading westward—his direction. All he needed was a ship to take him to the coast. This could be his chance to capture his prey.

With no time to spare, he jumped to his feet and retrieved the sapphire that Master Yiranor had given him. Wrapping it in a velvet cloth, he placed it carefully in the pocket of his bright red robe. On his desk lay a small glass orb, which would work nicely for transporting the visions in the flames. Holding the orb in front of him, he drew a portion of the fire into it. Quickly peering inside, he confirmed that the vision was still active. He felt a sense of relief. *At least that part has gone right.*

Running up the spiral staircase, he quickly removed the magical barriers from his vault. Transportation at this hour of the night could cost him dearly, but there was no time to waste haggling prices. Grabbing a large leather purse full of gold coins, he secured it to his belt. *If that doesn't cover the cost, I'll strangle the ship's captain.*

Hurrying down the stairs, he finally made it to the bottom. Seven floors felt like a hundred, as he knew each second was precious. Any delay could cost him this chance, which might never come again. He had to reach the coast as soon as possible.

Outside all was still. Only the sound of Telorithan's boots against the cobblestone path broke through the silence. The docks were not far from his tower, and he desperately hoped a ship would be ready to leave when he got there.

Upon reaching the docks, he could see figures moving about on one of the smaller ships. Hopefully a smaller vessel could move more quickly than a large one. Marching up the ramp to the boat's deck, he approached one of the sailors.

"You there," he said, his voice full of authority. "I need to book passage."

"We sail at sunrise," the shirtless elf replied. "You can pay the fare now if you like."

"I must leave at once," Telorithan declared. He untied the purse from his belt and presented it before the sailor. Giving it a shake, the coins inside jingled against one another. The sailor eyed him suspiciously.

"Gold," Telorithan stated forcefully. "All of it is yours if we leave immediately."

The sailor snatched the purse away from the silver-haired sorcerer. As he looked inside, his eyes filled with greed. "Oy!" he shouted to his shipmates. "Make ready to sail now!"

The others looked at him in confusion. "What are you talking about?" an elf carrying a load of rope asked.

"The captain will be wanting to shove off immediately when I show him this." He dangled the purse in front of the sailor, who apparently got the message. Dropping the rope to the deck, he raced over to begin pulling up the anchor.

"Make yourself at home," the elf said. Reaching inside the purse, he pulled out a few coins and slipped them into his pocket. The rest would be plenty to give to the captain. He disappeared out of sight below deck.

The rest of the sailors rushed to their duties to prepare the ship for departure. Telorithan took a seat near the starboard side of the craft, his anxiety rising. His fingers danced lightly over the sapphire in his pocket. Soon it would be filled with immense power. His mouth watered with anticipation.

Reaching into his other pocket, he pulled out the orb to check on his quarry once more. The soft orange glow gave way to a clear picture of the three companions. It appeared they were making camp near the coastline. He could not be certain where they were heading. All he could do was hope that he would reach them in time. If they moved away from the water, his journey would be for naught. He must not miss this perfect opportunity. Power surged through his veins, readying itself for the fight ahead.

Chapter 32

At the end of a second day of strenuous travel, the trio came within sight of the ocean. Descending one last grass-covered hill was all that was needed to bring them to the coastline. The sun was setting fast, and they would have to make camp for the night. If River was going into the sea, he would have to wait until first light. His companions would never let him wander away in the darkness

Kaiya looked back up the hill at the path they had taken. "It won't be as easy going back up," she commented.

"Maybe you can summon a hurricane to blow us back to the village," Galen replied with a mischievous grin.

"If only," she said.

River touched a hand to his forehead, wrinkling his brow as if in pain. Galen noticed his friend's discomfort.

"Are you all right?" he asked.

"Yes," River replied. "There are so many voices."

Galen looked at Kaiya, who looked around behind her to see if anyone was there. It was clear that neither of them were hearing the voices that River could hear.

"The sea has many voices," he explained. He took a seat on the grassy slope and stared out over the water. Still feeling as though someone were watching him, he chose not to relay the matter to his companions. They had already expressed their concern for his entering the water alone, and he had no desire to trouble them further. Most of the day's conversation had been kept light, and he hoped to continue the trend into the night.

"Let's make camp," Kaiya said, taking out her blanket. The air at this elevation was warmer, but a chilly breeze still came from the mountains.

They built a small fire, and it wasn't long before Kaiya and Galen fell asleep. After an exhausting day of walking over rough terrain, they had little energy left for anything else. As his companions slept beneath the stars, River remained awake, listening to the voices of the ocean. He felt a strong compulsion to enter the water, but he refrained. His companions would be frantic if they awoke to find him missing. For their sake, he remained close by the fire. After a while, he drifted off to sleep as well.

In a dream, he saw the ocean. Its magnificent blue spread before him, the brightness of day reflecting in its waves. Before his eyes, the blue faded and was replaced with an orange glow. The surface of the water caught fire, and all before him was engulfed in flames. The fire leapt toward the sky, leaving behind nothing but black smoke.

Shielding his eyes, he dropped to his knees, coughing. Squinting, he tried to make out the figure approaching him. Whoever it was meant to do him great harm. The strength of magic within this person was unmistakably strong. Before River could react, a great downpour doused the flames, and the wind blew the figure from view. River was alone once again, staring out onto the blue of the ocean.

At the first light of dawn, River awoke. He felt surprisingly calm after his strange dream. Sitting up, he did not feel any magical presence that had not been there before. His companions were still sleeping as he looked upon the sea. The deep-blue coloration was intact, and nothing seemed out of the ordinary. The weather was fine, and there was no hint of any impending storm. He shrugged the dream away, thinking it to be nothing significant. In the back of his mind, he still felt as if someone were watching. Perhaps it was Ryllak, still worrying for his safety and nothing more.

With the sun shining down on her face, Kaiya finally awoke. She sat up to see River already up, but Galen was still fast asleep. Tossing her blanket aside, she stretched her arms and gave a final yawn before rising to her feet. Giving Galen a nudge with her toe, she said, "Wake up!"

He startled from his sleep and glared at Kaiya. Squinting his eyes from the morning light, he tried to roll over and return to his dreams. Kaiya wouldn't hear of it. She pulled the blanket away from him and tossed it to the side.

"Come on, get up," she said.

Slowly, he lifted himself from the ground and brushed the dust from his charcoal-gray robe. Taking in a deep breath, he let out a long sigh.

"Not much of a morning person, are you?" Kaiya asked, laughing.

He grunted.

242

"I'm ready to enter the water," River declared. "I don't know how long I'll be."

"We'll walk to the coastline with you," Kaiya replied.

The trio made their way along the beach, a cool breeze greeting them from the sea. The waves splashed gently upon the wet sand, leaving behind a faint trail of white foam. A white seabird drifted lazily on the breeze, his piercing call seeming to go on for miles.

"Did you bring a bathing suit?" Galen joked.

Smiling kindly at his friend, River said, "I'm afraid I'll have to go as I am."

"We'll be waiting for you," Kaiya said. "Good luck." She wasn't sure what else to say. Not knowing where the opal would be found, she couldn't offer any real advice. Though she'd been to this beach before, she rarely entered the water. She wasn't a strong swimmer, and she certainly couldn't go to the bottom. It was curious that River didn't seem nervous. Even someone like him surely couldn't feel at home at the bottom of an ocean.

Galen seemed to be reading her thoughts. With a laugh, he said, "Don't get too comfortable down there. You might not want to come back."

River dismissed the joke. "The water is a part of me, but I belong in the Vale. I'll see you both soon."

With those words he slowly walked into the surf and disappeared beneath the blue. Galen and Kaiya watched, wondering if he might resurface immediately. Perhaps he would find the artifact as soon as he was submerged. Nearly half an hour passed before either of them spoke.

Finally, Kaiya broke the silence. "I guess this might take a while. What shall we do to pass the time?"

"Let's have a walk along the beach," Galen said, staring off into the distance. "There's a patch of trees not too far away. Let's go and have a look." Galen had never been outside the Vale, and he was interested to see more of the landscape.

"I've never been much past here," Kaiya admitted. She had only traveled to this beach with her father to meet merchant ships. They used to sell wool to customers in the Sunswept Isles, but the trade had ended some years ago. The Enlightened Elves did not like depending on others for anything, and they preferred dealing with their own kind instead of the dwarves.

"It will be an adventure for both of us then," Galen said. "Let's go."

Taking one last look at the ocean where River had gone under, Kaiya checked to see if he was returning. Seeing no sign of him, she nodded to Galen. They walked along the sand and enjoyed the salty fragrance of the sea. The forested area was only a few miles away, and Kaiya wondered if it was the same forest that would eventually lead to the Vale.

"Is this the way to your home?" she asked.

"Not really," he replied. "You'd have to stick to the mountain's base and follow it to the Vale. It would probably take three of four days, but I'm not really sure. I've never been this way, and I don't often look at maps."

The beach stretched on endlessly before them. After a while, they turned away from the ocean, bound for the forest in the distance. The tall trees stood menacingly, hiding the dangers inside.

Chapter 33

Despite being pelted with saltwater spray from the speeding ship, Telorithan leaned heavily upon the side rail. The orb in his hand was warm, and he could sense himself coming closer to his prey. As they continued toward the shore, he noticed a change within the orb. Peering inside, he saw River entering the ocean and slipping beneath the blue. *Where is he going?*

The orb's orange glow faded as his target moved farther from its gaze, hidden within the deep expanse of the ocean. Striding to the front of the ship, he held the orb out into the wind. As it shimmered, he changed directions until the flames within became red.

"Sailor," he called to one of the elves behind him. "We must change course. Head northwest to those islands." He pointed into the distance where three tiny islands jutted above the waves.

The sailor nodded and ran to inform the captain of his passenger's request. Only a moment later, the captain himself came to speak with the sorcerer. His skin was darkened and rough from many years beneath the sun, and his dirty brown hair was cut short.

"We'll lose speed heading that way," he said. "There's a reef that we'll need to avoid."

"I must reach those islands," Telorithan insisted, staring into his orb. The elemental was heading straight for those islands. It was alone, and the second presence was nowhere nearby. His body tensed in anticipation. He could almost feel the elemental's power within his grasp.

The captain signaled his steersman to change course and the ship slowed almost instantly. Ships from the Sunswept Isles used special enchantments to allow them more speed and to aid their travel against the wind, but they did nothing to protect a ship from a reef. They would have to proceed with caution.

"We won't be able to drop anchor there. You'll have to take a rowboat if you intend to set foot on those islands."

Telorithan shot the captain a hateful look but knew there was no use arguing. The ship was far too large to make it over the reef, and he could not waste his magic for travel.

"Fine," he grumbled, making his way to a row of small boats tethered on the deck.

With the help of two sailors, Telorithan climbed inside and was lowered to the water's surface. "Return for me before nightfall," he instructed them. "If you don't, there will be trouble." His eyes flashed red, and the young sailor nodded quickly.

The ship turned away from the reef, and Telorithan began to row. He was less than a mile from the island, and the orb still buzzed with activity as it sat upon his lap. The elemental was close. He did not yet know how he would convince it to surface, nor did he know the creature's purpose in coming here. Though he had no idea what it was searching for beneath the waves, he hoped that being bound in an elf body would force it to come to the surface for air.

I will not fail.

Coming ashore, he paced back and forth across the sand. Noticing this anxious activity, he forced himself to stop and took a seat upon one of the many large stones littering the island's surface. He did his best to clear his mind, focusing only on his own energy. Drawing in a deep breath, he held it for a second before releasing it. As he stared into the orb, he willed the elemental to come to him. *Here is what you seek.*

* * * * *

Hundreds of feet below the surface, River glided through the depths. To his relief, salt water was as easy to maneuver through as fresh water. He had expected it to be different from what he was used to, but he felt as natural here as he did in the Blue River of the Vale. Within the ocean were thousands of water elementals. In his elf form, he wondered if any of them would know him or consider him their kin. With luck, one of them might come near and help him in his search for the artifact.

All manner of life greeted his sight as he searched for the opal. A school of small yellow fish played in the bubbles created by a giant clam's vibrant purple lips. An octopus scurried away from River's shadow, hiding itself in a tiny opening in the coral. Some of the fish seemed curious about his presence, a few of them nipping gently at his robe. In his heart, he wished he had time to explore and take in the wonders of the sea.

That would have to wait for another time, though. Today he must find the opal and return to the dwarf village as quickly as possible. Lives were depending on him, and he had no time for play.

In the distance, he spotted what appeared to be a drop-off and possibly an underwater cave. That seemed a likely hiding place for an artifact that didn't want to be found. As he rotated in the water to investigate the area, he felt the presence of magic pulling at him. It was not, however, coming from the direction of the cave. What he felt was coming from the opposite direction. Beyond the reef, there was shallow water that came up to a sandbar. There might even be a small island nearby. *Would the ancients have hidden it on land?* The only information the Spirit had given him was a vision of this area. He had assumed the opal still rested at the bottom, but perhaps it was on a beach or had long since embedded itself within the coral.

The presence of magic was unmistakable. Energy was radiating toward him, calling him to join it. Taking a last look at the caves, he decided to follow the magic. It was an artifact of great power that he was seeking. Surely its presence would be easily felt by someone like him.

Making his way to the sandbar, he paused for a moment. He knew he was only a half-day's journey by sea from the Sunswept Isles. If this was indeed the artifact he was sensing, why had the Enlightened Elves allowed it to sit idle for so long? Their race highly prized magic, and they would most likely kill each other to possess such a powerful item. Of course it was possible that none of them could sense it. Perhaps it took the skills of an elemental or a closer bloodline to the ancients themselves.

Being of the race of First Ones gave River an inborn magical ability that was alien to the Enlightened Elves. All of them could perform some minor spells, but it took immense study to master a single form of elemental magic. The determined ones spent centuries studying to earn the rank of Master. They were held in the highest regard by all those beneath them, and the elite rank was required to hold any position in their government.

In contrast, the Westerling Elves learned magic easily. Their close connection to the earth itself granted them this gift, but that did not make them more powerful than their island kin. The Enlightened Elves who became Masters would be formidable opponents should they choose to be. Westerling Elves did not focus on any type of magic that could bring about destruction. Instead they focused on sustaining life, and protecting the land and creatures around them.

The pull of magic became stronger as he reached the sandbar, and he decided he must investigate. It was entirely possible that no Enlightened Elf with the skill to detect it had happened upon the artifact. It was also possible that none of them had the ability to sense it at all. Determined to find out what he was sensing, River brought his head above the surface of the water. Indeed, there was an island before him. There were no trees, only an abundance of cold, jagged rocks. The presence of magic was unmistakable, and his hopes were high that he would soon be heading back with the opal.

Chapter 34

When Kaiya and Galen reached the trees, they looked upon massive evergreens towering high into the air. These were ancient trees that had grown in the millennia before humans or dwarves came to inhabit the world. Only the First Ones had been present when these trees were small. The ancients had tended this forest before crossing over. Now, they were part of the Wildlands, the untamed region of Nōl'Deron.

Kaiya tilted her head back to view the treetops as they reached the sky. "I can't believe I never came here before. I was only a few miles away, and I missed seeing this."

Galen replied, "We have more lovely trees in the Vale. They're silver and wide enough to build a home inside." He looked down at her, his face shining. "You should come and see them."

"I might just do that," she replied, still staring skyward.

"Shall we venture in?" Galen asked.

Kaiya nodded, and the pair stepped cautiously into the forest. The ground was littered with fallen needles and pinecones. A strong woody scent filled the air. All was silent except for the occasional rustling of a branch, where small furry creatures scurried about. Smaller trees and bushes were scattered randomly through the forest, adding to its feral appearance. There were no visible paths or signs of habitation.

"Does anyone live here?" Kaiya asked.

"I don't know," Galen replied. "Maybe."

It was cooler within the forest than on the beach, and the sunlight was mostly hidden behind the massive boughs of the evergreens. It was as if twilight had come early, despite being bright and sunny only a few steps away.

"We should probably turn back," Kaiya suggested. "I don't want River to wonder where we've gone."

Before he could reply, Galen felt a sharp pain. Looking down, he saw a feathered arrow protruding from the left side of his chest. Kaiya gasped as he was struck, pulling him to the ground to cover him. Galen buckled to his knees and remained motionless, stunned by the sudden attack.

Kaiya scanned the trees and caught sight of a second arrow making its way toward her. With a flash of her gray eyes, she altered its course, blowing it away with a small gust of wind. Two elves hopped out of a low tree, their bows held at the ready.

"Why have you attacked my friend?" she demanded. "We did nothing to you!" She was visibly angry, her fists clenched and her body quaking with rage.

"You're in our territory, and you're not welcome here," one of them said. He was much shorter than Galen, shirtless, and wore red paint upon his face. His skin was darkened from the sun, and his dirty blond hair was spiked in a thin strip on top of his head. Raising his bow to take aim, he said, "It's time to finish the job."

Before he could loose another arrow, Kaiya summoned her strength and knocked him backward. He stumbled off-balance and hit the ground with a thud, dropping his bow. His friend tried to grab Kaiya by the arm, but his movements were too slow. Her eyes flashed silver as she knocked him back with a gust of air.

Previously unseen elves descended the trees and circled around Kaiya. Turning to check on Galen, she laid a hand on his cheek. His face was pale, and his breath was coming in shallow spurts. Despite his pain, he managed a weak smile. Staring into his dark eyes for only a moment, her heart ached. *I cannot let them hurt him again*, she thought.

The elves moved in closer, their bows drawn. Kaiya closed her eyes and slowly raised both arms toward the sky. Feeling the charge in the air, she knew the magic had worked. With a quick movement of her arms, she called down the lightning. Directing the blast at the elves, she scattered them and singed a few as well. Having never witnessed such a spectacle, most of them ran for their lives. A few stood motionless, staring at the dwarf who could summon energy from the sky.

Kaiya had no patience for the gawkers, and she did not feel safe with them around. Mustering the wind to her aid, she attacked. With a flash of silver in her eyes, she summoned a gale that blew the elves off their feet and sent them tumbling through the forest.

Crouching next to Galen, she asked, "Can you walk?"

He nodded, and she helped him to his feet. She stood only to the height of his waist, which made her a rather awkward crutch. He leaned heavily on her shoulder with his left hand and clutched at the arrow with his right. Slowly, they emerged from the forest, finding the sunlight again on the beach.

Kaiya led Galen around a cluster of boulders that she hoped would shield them from the eyes of the forest elves. He leaned upon one of the rocks and coughed, unable to take in a full breath.

"Try to stay calm," Kaiya said. She had no medical training and no idea how to treat a wound such as this.

Leaning his head back on a rock, he coughed a few more times. His right hand still clutched at the arrow, but he did not have the courage to pull it out. "You'll have...to...," he tried to say.

Kaiya knew what he meant. He wanted her to remove the arrow from his chest. Pulling it out, however, could cause him to bleed to death. Sometimes it was best to leave it in. She knew that much, but that was the extent of her medical knowledge. The worst she had ever treated were scrapes and cuts. This was a serious wound, one that could prove fatal.

She swallowed hard and looked around the boulder to make sure no elves had followed them. Seeing no one there, she felt a small amount of relief. Turning her focus back to the arrow, she reached a hand for its shaft. She hesitated before gripping it, fearing she would do more harm than good.

Galen looked at her and gave a weak nod. "You must," he whispered.

Chapter 35

Though he'd been away only a few days, Lenora

found herself missing River more and more. Each day without him helped her realize how much she cared for him. She had plenty of work to occupy her time, but at the back of her mind, his absence was certainly noticed.

Each day more patients arrived for treatment at the hospital. Though she could not cure them, Lenora's newest herb concoction had done wonders for easing their symptoms. Many of them were able to leave the hospital after only a single night's stay. As luck would have it, the herbs she required were in good supply in the mountain village. It was summer in the mountains, and yellowroot, sage, and ginger were growing in abundance. Cloves were the only necessary herb the dwarves did not grow themselves. Luckily, they were quite popular in dwarven kitchens, being one of the herbs they traded for with the merchants from the Kingdom of Al'marr.

Despite her new remedy, the hospital was still full of ailing dwarves. Some of them simply did not respond to the treatment. Others, it seemed, waited too long to come to her, and their symptoms had grown worse. There had been no new deaths this day, but she feared that would not last. Even with her best efforts, some of the patients were still growing weaker.

Ortin the smith was among those lying on a cot in the hospital. Like many, he had waited to seek treatment until he was seriously ill. He went about his work as usual until he could no longer stand. One of his customers found him lying on the ground unconscious and brought him in for care. The herbs helped with his cough, but his fever refused to subside.

Kassie had declared Ortin to be the grumpiest patient she had dealt with. When he was awake, he was loud and demanding. She strongly preferred the moments when he would sleep, but he occasionally woke in a rage. The fever had taken hold of his mind, and his situation was critical.

Lenora showed surprising patience with him. Though he was ungrateful and often obnoxious, she sympathized with his condition. She had tried several different herbal remedies, but none of them brought his fever down for any significant amount of time. Today, he had been silent. She caught only a glimpse of him awake when he was shivering and mumbling to himself.

Lenora sat next to Kassie, who was grinding more herbs for a potion. Lenora could not decide what to try next for Ortin, and she sat with her head in her hands.

"You aren't getting enough rest," Kassie said. "Why don't you take an hour or two for a nap?"

Lenora looked into Kassie's kind, motherly eyes. "I'll be all right," she insisted.

Grabbing a phial from the desk, Lenora slowly walked to Ortin's cot. He laid motionless, beads of sweat covering his forehead. Sitting next to him, she gently lifted his head with her hand.

"Drink," she said softly.

Ortin roused from his sleep to take a sip of the medicine. "Awful," he grumbled, letting half the liquid dribble down his beard.

"You must drink," she said, tilting the phial once more to his lips.

Before he could protest, his body shook uncontrollably. Lenora jumped to her feet and placed one hand on his forehead, the other on his chest. Closing her eyes, she spread white magic throughout his body. The shaking subsided, and he looked at her in amazement.

"What did you do?" he asked, his voice full of vigor. Propping himself up on his elbows, he stared into Lenora's eyes.

"I've used magic to help you," she replied with a tired smile. Lenora did not have enough magic to treat all the patients, so she reserved it for only the most dire cases. Fearing that Ortin might not survive the seizures, she had chosen to use a significant portion of her magical reserves to treat him.

"I feel better than I have in days," he said, the surprise audible in his voice.

"Your fever is gone," she said. "You should get some rest."

"I don't feel the need to rest anymore," he replied. "You've cured me."

"It's not a cure, I'm afraid. I've only treated your symptoms. They could return, and you should get some rest while you can."

Taking Lenora's hand, he sat up on the cot. "Name your reward, my lady. You have given me back my life, and I would thank you."

"You can reward me by taking care of yourself," she replied. "You are well enough to leave the hospital for now if you wish, but you must return the minute you feel the symptoms returning. Treating this condition early seems to be the only way of keeping it under control."

"I will do as you command," he replied. "But I would still have you name a reward. There is no better craftsman in these mountains than myself. I can craft you anything, big or small. Please, my lady, I insist."

Seeing that Ortin was sincere, she gave the matter some thought. She would rather not accept payment for her services, but she did not want to insult him by refusing a gift. Her mind wandered to thoughts of River and the ocean, and she knew what she would ask for. "Could you craft a ring with a blue stone?" she asked.

"My lady, you shall have the finest ring any lady ever wore." His eyes sparkled as he made the promise.

"I'd like you to make it for my dearest friend, River," she replied, blushing slightly.

"I see," he said, noticing her shy smile. "He is special to you, so I'll make him a ring with the bluest sapphire the mountains can provide." He hopped off the cot and kissed Lenora's hand before hurrying out of the tent to begin his work.

Lenora sat down again next to Kassie, who had been listening to their conversation.

"A ring for your friend?" she asked. "You two are in love, aren't you?" She nudged Lenora with her elbow.

"I think I do love him," Lenora admitted. "I find myself hardly able to concentrate now that he is away."

"That's how it starts," Kassie replied knowingly. "I haven't forgotten what it was like to be young and in love." She patted Lenora's arm and said, "Don't worry, dear. He'll be back soon."

"I hope you're right," Lenora replied.

Chapter 36

Emerging from the water, River stepped onto the island. The presence of magic was unmistakable. Certain that the artifact must be nearby, he searched the ground. All around his feet, the sand was littered with tiny broken shells and numerous rocks. Staring intently at the ground, he had no idea that someone was near.

Seated comfortably behind a boulder, Telorithan had been awaiting the elemental's arrival. Hearing him step onto the shore, he rose to greet his prey. "We meet at last," he said.

River looked up, surprised to hear a voice. There was no settlement nearby, and there did not seem to be any reason why someone would travel to this island. An Enlightened Elf stood before him, equal to him in height. His skin was bronze, his hair silver, and his eyes a brilliant blue. He wore a dark-red robe, suggesting his skill with fire magic. One hand cradled a glowing orange orb. River observed him closely and remained silent.

As he stared into River's sapphire eyes, Telorithan could sense his power. The feeling was as strong as any fire elemental he had encountered on the Red Isle. For a moment, he feared this elemental might not be inhibited by his elf form, and a shiver made its way down his spine.

"Mistonwey," Telorithan uttered. Sensing the power of the ancient God of the Rivers, he hoped he had the ability to tame him.

"You may call me River," he replied. River's gaze penetrated Telorithan's mind. A faint line of blue magic emitted from his hand as he held it forth in greeting. "Lorith," he said.

"My name is Telorithan," he replied, insulted. No one had called him Lorith since his childhood. He had taken the longer name to emulate the name of the ancient gods. Only they possessed the power he craved, and he insisted on being called by a more fitting name than the one given to him by his parents.

"You will never succeed in binding a god," River stated matter-of-factly. "You are an Island Dweller, and you will age. To accomplish such a feat, you would have to be one of the First Ones. We are ageless, you are not."

Angered by his words, Telorithan replied, "You will see that I am no mere mortal!" Raising his hands, he blasted red fire at River. Without hesitation, River lifted a blue magical shield to protect himself. The shield absorbed Telorithan's magic entirely, leaving River unharmed.

"Cease these games and prove yourself a worthy opponent!" Telorithan spat.

"I have no desire to fight you," River replied calmly. "Leave this place, and I will forget this incident." He did not fully realize the danger he was in or Telorithan's desperation.

Determined to capture the elemental's essence, the sorcerer attacked again. With a blast of energy, he knocked an unprepared River off his feet. Hitting the ground hard, River realized that the elf meant him serious harm. Without understanding what a fire mage would want from a water elemental, he shielded himself once more.

Telorithan continued to attack, throwing fire and energy at River. All of the magic was absorbed into the shield, further angering the sorcerer. He had faced several opponents in the dueling arena of the Sunswept Isles, and his attacks had always been enough to penetrate a shield. He could not understand why he was failing now. Water, being what he considered the weakest element, was usually the easiest for him to defeat. This time was different.

Reaching into the pocket of his robe, he pulled out the large sapphire he had prepared to contain River's essence. Once the elemental could see he was prepared, perhaps it would strike fear into his heart and cause him to falter.

River looked at the sapphire that was prepared to hold his essence. "What makes you think you can control water?" he asked, still maintaining his shield.

"I have mastered fire," the sorcerer replied. "I will master you."

Once again Telorithan attacked. This time, he focused his full mind on tearing down River's shield. Fire could evaporate water, leaving the elf defenseless. With a burst of flames summoned from his fingertips, he blasted River's shield. River, whose years of training were trivial compared to those of his opponent, was unable to maintain his defense. His shield evaporated before his eyes, leaving him vulnerable to attack.

Summoning a blast of energy, Telorithan pummeled River, knocking him into the rocks. When he landed, River realized the gravity of his situation. This elf would indeed kill him if he had the chance, and his essence would be bound in eternal torment. Though his body was bruised, he still had an immense supply of magic. Summoning his resolve, he blasted blue fire at his opponent, hoping to stop the attack.

Telorithan was prepared for River's counterstrike. Knowing he could leach power from regular elves, he was determined to do so with this elf as well. Being an elemental would only mean a greater power store, and Telorithan was determined to have it. With one hand, he blocked River's attack, and with the other, he focused his energy on draining the elemental's power.

River could feel power leaving his body, and it caught him by surprise. This was a skill he had never heard of, and certainly not one that he would use. Having no idea how to defend against it, he tried in vain to summon his shield. Telorithan's power was too strong, and River could barely move. Closing his eyes, he reached for his small supply of remaining magic and steeled himself against the attack. With every ounce of strength, he willed his magic to obey.

River's body glowed with a pale blue light. Telorithan noticed, but he did not pause in his attack. To break his spell now would be folly. He was determined to drain every drop of magic from the elemental's supply. In such a weakened state, it would then be possible to bind him.

River's body continued to glow as he concentrated on breaking through Telorithan's spell. The light became brighter until a sudden flash knocked both elves backward. The draining spell had been broken, burning the hands of its caster. River stumbled over the rocks as he fell and landed in the water. Feeling himself freed from the sorcerer's grasp, he used the small amount of energy remaining to him to dive down into the blue.

Telorithan would not let his prey escape so easily. With his opponent's power augmenting his own supply, he was determined to find him at any cost. The elf's essence would be his, and he would be one step closer to binding a god.

Chapter 37

With one quick motion, Kaiya grabbed the arrow and pulled it from Galen's chest. He gave a loud groan as the arrow was removed, his body tensing from the pain. The wound was bleeding heavily, and she instinctively pressed both hands against it to staunch the flow.

"I'm sorry," she said, wrinkling her brow. She had no way of numbing the pain he was in, and she hoped she had made the right choice in removing the arrow.

Galen closed his eyes to rest for a moment and found that his breathing was coming a bit easier. Still he was able to take only shallow breaths, but the sharp pain he had felt with each gulp of air was not nearly as strong. Opening his eyes, he looked at Kaiya's tear-stained face. Despite her eyes being reddened, he found her to be quite lovely. There was great kindness and also sadness in her eyes, and he wondered why he hadn't seen it before.

Noticing that he was looking at her, she asked, "Are you in much pain?"

He shook his head. "It's better now."

Lifting her hands slightly, Kaiya could see that the wound had not begun to clot. She hoped that applying pressure would quicken the process, but the blood came as quickly as ever. Securing both hands over the wound, she closed her eyes to concentrate. River had said she could create fire by pulling the heat from the air. She had no desire to light Galen on fire, but she might be able to use the heat to seal the wound.

A soft breeze was blowing from the ocean, and Kaiya focused her mind to it. The breeze was heated by the sun's rays, which traveled uninhibited through the cloudless sky. Willing the heat to her fingertips, she transferred it into the wound. She could feel the heat against her hands, and Galen gave a few grunts suggesting he felt it as well. Removing her hands from his chest, she could see the bleeding had stopped.

A smile of relief spread across her face, and she finally let out the breath she had been holding. Galen opened his eyes to meet hers, and she saw that his mischievous nature had not been injured. He grinned at her as best he could.

"For a minute I thought you didn't want to take your hands off me," he said.

She shook her head, dismissing the comment. "How do you feel?"

"Better," he replied. He reached out slowly to take her hand and pressed it to his lips. "Thank you," he said, looking deep into her eyes.

Feeling slightly embarrassed by the look he was giving her, she pulled her hand away and blushed. She hadn't noticed before how handsome he was, nor had she seen the mystery in his dark eyes. His countenance was warm, and her heart fluttered as she looked up to see he was still staring at her.

"Who were those elves?" Kaiya asked, hoping to avoid an awkward situation.

"The Young Ones," Galen replied quietly. "Also known as the Woodland Elves. Humans usually refer to them as Wild Elves. I guess we found out why." He tried to laugh but began coughing instead.

Worried, Kaiya said, "We should try to get back where we left River. I'm sure he'll be returning soon, and we'll want to get back right away. Lenora will be able to heal you." She spoke more to convince herself than him.

She helped him to his feet, and once again they started to walk. Their pace was slow, and Kaiya struggled to bear a portion of his weight upon her shoulder. She wished with all her being that she could fly upon the wind and carry him back to her village. Unfortunately, she had no idea if such a thing were even possible. The wind had never offered any guidance as far as flying was concerned.

Together they trudged along the beach, making their way slowly back to the spot where River had gone into the ocean. It was already afternoon by the time they arrived, and Galen was clearly exhausted. Kaiya helped him prop himself next to some rocks near the hillside. His breath was still shallow, and he hadn't spoken since they started walking. Kaiya worried his injury was greater on the inside, and she could do nothing to heal it.

She rubbed at her aching shoulder as she looked back over the ocean. Somewhere in the depths was River, and she hoped he would return soon. Without him, she had no idea if she would be able to get Galen back to her village in time. For all she knew, his wound could prove fatal.

Impatient for River's return, she tried to force herself to relax. Taking a seat next to Galen, she asked, "Are you feeling any better?" She placed a hand gently on his face, brushing his hair away from his eyes.

"I'll be all right," he said softly. "It doesn't hurt as much. I'm just tired."

Kaiya wondered how long she should wait for River. It could be days before he returned. She knew he would continue searching for the opal until he found it, even if it took a month. He had no way of knowing that his cousin had been hurt, and Kaiya did not know how to contact him.

"Is there any way to get a message to River?" she asked.

Galen thought for a moment and smiled. "You could try sticking your head in the water and shouting."

Kaiya shook her head. At least his sense of humor was still intact, even if he was in pain. Making up her mind, she said, "We have to get you back to the village. We don't know how long he will be, and you need treatment."

"No," Galen replied. "I'll be fine, really. Let's wait a bit. I'm too tired to walk right now anyway."

His response made Kaiya uneasy. His fatigue could be a sign that he wasn't going to be all right. The thought of losing him made her heart ache. Kneeling next to him, she cradled his head on her shoulder and held him tightly. Her tears flowed down her cheeks, falling silently to the sand.

A change in the wind startled her to action. Climbing back to her feet, she left Galen lying peacefully on the beach while she approached the shoreline. *River's in trouble,* she realized. The magic she sensed on the wind was not only his. Somewhere beyond the blue he was being attacked, and she could feel it.

The voice on the wind came loud and clear. *He will not survive without you.*

Forgetting everything else, she closed her eyes and focused her mind on the wind. Mustering every ounce of strength in her body, she unleashed the fury of the wind and cast it at River's attacker. With her mind, she homed in on his location, sending the air to subdue him. Her eyes shot open, shimmering with silver light. Sparks of energy shot from her fingertips, flying unrestrained above the water. Her target had no warning that he was about to feel the wrath of the wind.

Chapter 38

Diving down into the blue, River could hear the voices of other elementals in the ocean. They were calling to him, rejuvenating his power. On the island above, Telorithan was trying with all his might to raise River from the sea, but the combined power of the elementals prevented his spell from working. River's power was quickly being restored, his full strength returning.

Telorithan could see that his magic was failing to penetrate the surface of the water. He created only a small disturbance at the surface as he attempted to force the elemental back within his reach. "No!" he cried, fearing that the elemental would escape. "I will not fail!"

Suddenly, a gust of wind struck him, stealing his breath and forcing him to his knees. As he doubled over and tried to collect his wits, a second gust of wind struck him in a frontal assault. Landing flat on his back, his head struck a rock. Crimson blood seeped from the gash, staining his silver hair.

Placing his hand against his head to stop the blood, his anger rose. Scrambling to his feet, he summoned his power in time to block a third gust of wind. The blow struck him, and he felt as if a stone had hit him in the chest. This time, however, he remained standing. His confidence building, he reached deep within himself into his stolen stores of magic. Across the sea, he sensed the sorcerer who had conjured the wind. This newcomer's power rivaled that of the elemental, and he remembered the second magical being he had sensed before coming to this place. Apparently the elemental's magical companion was nearby, and Telorithan would have to face them both.

He felt a sudden wave of fear and hoped that River would stay below, fleeing for his pitiful life. He would succeed only if he could handle each of them individually. Scrambling for his orb, he gazed into the flames and willed them to move toward the coast. Two figures were present, one lying motionless on the beach, the other standing at the ready at the coastline. *The dwarf girl? How can this be?*

Her eyes flashed with silver magic, sparks gracing her fingertips. Telorithan could not believe what he was witnessing. The magic he had sensed all along was coming from a dwarf. Not just any dwarf, either. This was an insignificant female. This creature had far stronger magic than the majority of Enlightened Elves.

In his distraction, Telorithan did not see the next blow before it hit him. Silver sparks rained down, jolting and twisting his body as he crashed to the sand. Severe pain ran through him, and he cried out in agony. Before he could regain control, a second wave of energy hit him. Silver bolts of lightning struck him, holding him firm within their grasp. He could feel his power draining, flying skyward in tiny droplets of silver light. Reaching out with a hand as if to catch them, he watched as they floated to the sky and dissolved into the clouds above.

As he lay powerless on the sand, River re-emerged from the sea. The ocean had restored him to full power, and he towered over Telorithan. The orb still clutched in one of his hands, the sorcerer crushed it, hoping to absorb the small amount of power left inside it. The glass cut his hand, but he felt nothing. His body was numb from the lightning that had drained his power. His only hope to avoid death was to find some way to continue fighting. Surely, this elemental would kill him if he could.

River encompassed Telorithan in blue magic, lifting him back to his feet. Telorithan attempted to lift his hands, but he was unable to move. He was held fast within the elemental's grasp.

"You are defeated," River said. "You will go back to your home and stop hunting me. Give up this scheme of yours to bind an elemental. If not, it will be your death."

Telorithan made no attempt to speak. Glaring at River, he knew he was defeated. His attempt had failed, but not because of his own weakness. He had underestimated the dwarf. Without her interference, he felt sure he would have bound River. If not for her, he would be on his way to the Red Isle to trap Yelaurad now. His dream could have come true this very day. *The dwarves will pay for this,* he swore.

River released the sorcerer, who slumped once again to his knees. The wind swirled around River, his dark hair dancing on the breeze. Looking back to the shore, he realized that Kaiya was there, helping him to subdue his attacker. She had completely drained Telorithan's power, saving River from a second fight when he returned to the island. Without her help, he wasn't sure he would have survived the encounter.

He looked upon the sorcerer with pity. Before him was an elf consumed by his own greed. His every thought was bent on achieving ultimate power. River could see his heart, and it was an empty void. No friendship dwelt inside, and there was no trace of love. River had no desire to end this elf's life. Instead, he would allow him to live the lonely life he had chosen for himself. There could be no greater punishment in River's mind.

The waves began to swell, fed by the summoned wind. Before his eyes, River saw a glimmer of white riding along a jet of water. With no further thought for Telorithan, he turned his attention to the sea. Diving back within the blue, he reached out to grasp the glistening gem. In his hand was the opal that would save the dwarves. Kaiya had forced the sea to give it up. With all speed, he swam back to her, hurried along by the wind.

Kaiya waved to him as he approached the shore. River smiled, opening his palm to show her the opal. It was larger than a duck's egg, and its smooth white surface shone with glimmers of pink, turquoise, and yellow.

With a shallow gasp, Kaiya reached out her hand to touch the cold surface of the stone. "It's beautiful," she said, her eyes reflecting its light. It vibrated slightly at her touch.

"Your people will be safe now," River replied.

"Galen is injured," she said. "He needs your help."

Hurrying to Galen's side, River asked, "What happened?"

"There were elves in that forest over there," Kaiya said, pointing to the tree line. "They shot him with an arrow. I removed it and stopped the bleeding, but he's still weak."

Galen managed a faint smile, his face pale. Keeping his eyes open felt like a chore. Without a word, River laid both hands on his friend's chest. Blue magic spread over Galen's body, and he took in a full breath for the first time since being shot. His eyes sparkled with a blue light for a moment, and he sat up with renewed vigor.

"What did you do?" he asked.

"I'm no healer," River replied. "I merely gave you some of the strength of my magic."

"Well, it feels great!" Galen said with a laugh.

Kaiya was overjoyed to see him restored to health. Forgetting herself, she threw her arms around him and kissed him. Backing off quickly, she looked down at the ground. "I'm sorry," she said. "I...,"

Galen's face lit up. "No need to apologize," he said. "If I'd known it would win me a kiss, I would have been injured sooner."

Kaiya looked away feeling embarrassed. It would be difficult for her to deny her feelings for Galen going forward.

River smiled warmly, approving of the match. "Perhaps Lenora will be happy to see me in one piece too," he commented. "We should head back. I've only given you temporary strength. It won't last."

The trio began their journey back to the mountains, leaving Telorithan behind on the island.

Chapter 39

Sitting motionless on the sand, Telorithan could sense River and the dwarf moving farther away. It would seem they had no interest in punishing him. *I've been a fool*, he realized. His entire life had been dedicated to the study of fire. What had made him think he could master water without so much as studying? The folly was all his own.

His thoughts turned to binding a fire elemental, the creature he should have been seeking in the first place. Sirra's knowledge of River's existence had prompted him to the wrong action. He blamed her for leading him astray. His intention had always been to truly master fire, and a water elemental did not fit into that equation.

No matter how long it took, he would dedicate himself to perfecting the binding process, and he would not make another attempt until he was confident in his ability to succeed. Failure was unacceptable, and he hated himself for listening to the enchantress. *She set me up for this failure, and I will not forget it.*

Hours passed as he sat upon the lonely island, contemplating his next move. Slowly, his magic stores regenerated as the sun moved lower in the sky. The ship would be returning soon to collect him. Not wanting them to see his disheveled appearance, Telorithan focused his magic to vanity. He removed the blood from his silver hair and concealed the cuts on his hand. After removing the sand and salt from his robe, he stood and looked toward the Sunswept Isles. They seemed smaller and even less significant than before.

Once I have achieved my mission, I will leave these isles.

Idly, he brushed his fingers through his silver strands. He regretted the movement of the ocean, which did not allow him to see his own reflection. As the ship came into sight, he used the small amount of magic remaining to him to cast a trivial spell that would give him a more pleasing appearance. Looking defeated was not an option, especially in front of elves who were so far beneath him.

Shoving his small boat into the water, he rowed past the reef to meet the ship. The sailors lowered a rope ladder for him to climb, and he made his way onto the deck. Without a word to any of them, he took a seat at the rear of the vessel and stared into the distance. The Red Isle lay to the north, waiting for him as always. Soon he would go there, and he would be triumphant. Then he would have his revenge on all those who had humiliated him this day.

* * * * *

Walking late into the night, River and his companions were determined to return to the dwarf village as quickly as possible. River hoped Lenora had the illness under control, but he knew she could not cure it without the opal. As they moved ever closer to the village, he could sense Indal's presence. Her angry mood had not changed, and he knew she would still refuse to leave willingly.

Galen was the first of the three to tire. His wound had not yet healed, and he needed rest before continuing the journey. Kaiya used the heat from the air to build a small fire before settling down to sleep. River kept watch a while before finally succumbing to sleep himself.

Early the next morning, they awoke to the sound of birdsong. The sun lifted itself over the horizon, filling the sky with pink light. With only a few short hours of sleep, they were determined to press on.

"How are you feeling this morning?" River asked Galen.

His breathing was shallow again, and the pain was evident on his face. "I've been better," he replied honestly.

River laid a hand on the wound, once again filling it with blue magic. Galen's pain subsided, and he felt rejuvenated and ready for travel.

"Thanks," Galen said with a smirk. "I'm beginning to like that spell."

The travelers set out once again, making their way along the mountainside. Kaiya was curious about the spell that had helped Galen. She walked alongside River, trying to figure out how he had accomplished what she could not.

"Is that elf magic?" she asked. "Or is that something I could learn to do as well?"

"From what I've seen of your abilities, I'm convinced you could learn anything," River replied. "I am only willing the magic to pass to him and give him strength. With practice, you should be able to do it as well."

"Feel free to practice on me whenever you like," Galen said.

Kaiya shook her head and looked at the ground. "You have magic too Galen, but you don't seem to use it often."

"I don't have skills like River," he admitted. "I'm not as good as Lenora either. I do have a few talents, but I reserve them for special occasions."

"Galen is a master of the archives," River said proudly. "He's highly respected among our people." He glanced over at Galen, who pretended not to notice the exaggeration.

"Archives?" Kaiya repeated. "You're a writer?"

Galen nodded. "I mainly write histories."

"You'll have to teach me some of your language," Kaiya replied. "Maybe Trin could teach you some of our ancient dialect."

"I'd be delighted to teach you," he replied. "And Trin has already shown me a few things. His work with runes is intriguing. Our people rarely write spells. They aren't normally spoken word, but rather something that is done silently in one's mind. The idea of etching a spell onto an item is fascinating." His voice revealed his sincere interest in the topic.

"I'm sure he'd love to teach you more," Kaiya said. "He could probably learn a few things from you as well. He's something of a loner, but I don't think he'd mind having you around." Her words revealed more about herself than Trin. Their journey was nearing its end, and she did not look forward to his departure back to the Vale.

They journeyed throughout the day, hurrying with every step.

"We should be nearing my house," Kaiya informed the others. "If we continue at this pace, we should be there a few hours after sunset. We can spend the night there and head for the village at first light."

The air grew thinner as they ascended higher into the mountains. The way was as rocky as before, but their steps felt lighter as they walked. Before, their journey had been full of questions and uncertainty. Now, they knew their destination, and they were returning in victory.

Near midnight they arrived at Kaiya's home. Doozle barked cautiously as they approached, but his expression turned to joy as they came into view. He greeted the trio excitedly, wagging his tail and licking their hands.

"It's good to see you too," Kaiya said, scratching him behind one ear.

Darvil heard the commotion and left his bed to see who was outside. On seeing his daughter, he rushed to meet her. Squeezing her tightly against his chest, he said, "I'm glad you're back, girl."

Squirming to release herself from his grip, she said, "Let's all get some sleep. We have a big day ahead of us tomorrow."

Chapter 40

Returning to his tower, Telorithan realized that nothing had changed. No one was aware of his failure, and the world carried on as normal. After a bath, he intended to begin studying right away. Another visit to Yiranor's library might be in order. There were many fire elementals present on the Red Isle. His failure against one of them might result in retaliation from the others, which meant he needed to learn how best to defend against them. If he succeeded, he expected the others would accept him as one of their own.

He had no intention of making the mistake of rushing into it again. Determined not to make another attempt until he was fully prepared, he dreaded the thought that it might be years before his goal was achieved. In addition, he would need to learn to wield the elemental's power before he could attempt the binding of the fire god. That could take even longer, perhaps centuries. He was not a patient elf, and the thought of all the work ahead of him was distressing.

As he ascended the spiral staircase to his library, a thought occurred to him. Two elements had come together to defeat him. He felt certain he would have succeeded in binding River had the dwarf not interfered. This gave him hope that he did indeed have the power to subdue a single elemental, but getting one alone could prove difficult. He had no idea why air and water would come together as allies, and he wondered who might come to the aid of a lone fire elemental. It was a possibility he intended to prepare for.

After a few hours of poring over scrolls, a knock came from his door. A servant poked his head inside, waiting for permission to speak.

"What is it?" Telorithan asked impatiently.

"It's Mistress Sirra," the servant replied. "She's come for a visit."

Annoyed, the sorcerer turned back to his scroll without saying a word. Suddenly, an idea came to his mind. He rose and proceeded to his laboratory to retrieve an item that could possibly save him years of study. Searching through a drawer, he smiled as his eyes fell onto the item he hoped to find. Inspecting it carefully, he slipped it into his pocket before making his way downstairs to greet his guest.

Sirra sat casually upon the velvet chair in Telorithan's sitting room. A goblet of wine dangled in one hand, and her raven hair fell loosely upon her breast. "I'm glad you didn't come to any harm," she said, a seductive smile on her lips. "I don't know what I would do without you."

Telorithan gazed at her with contempt. "I went unprepared," he replied.

Sirra laughed. "That's something of an understatement."

Not taking kindly to the comment, the sorcerer said, "Would you care to enlighten me?"

"Well," she began, "obviously this elf has true elemental powers. His form isn't holding him back at all. You may as well not have bothered."

Feeling his anger rise, he did his best to suppress it. "You expected me to fail?" Sirra was the one who had suggested he try binding this elemental, and now she was mocking him.

"You weren't able to trap an elderly master, so it stands to reason you couldn't trap a demigod," she replied. "It was a difficult task. It's to be expected that it would take more than one try. Next time you might do better."

"I intend to," he replied coldly. He fidgeted with the amethyst in his robe pocket, waiting for the perfect moment to strike.

"Come and sit," she said, patting the seat next to her. "We can discuss your next move if you like. Or we can do something else." Pursing her crimson lips, she blew a kiss his direction.

With a half-smile, he sat next to her and reached for the wine bottle. After pouring himself a drink, he took a sip and settled back in his seat. "I will not fail when it comes to trapping fire," he declared. "I've already figured out exactly what I need."

"Do tell," she said, feigning interest.

"You see, it took two different elements to subdue me. Water would not have succeeded without help from air. Their combined powers were overwhelming. I was not prepared for it."

"So you're planning to master a second element?" Sirra asked. "That will take a rather long time."

"No," he replied, sitting up straight. "A true mastery isn't necessary. I simply need to have it under my control."

"Which element did you have in mind?" she asked.

"Earth," he replied with a smile. Leaning forward, he kissed her lips. She welcomed his caress and moaned with pleasure.

"A wise decision," she said. "You happen to have an accomplished earth enchantress right next to you. Of course, I'm going to require payment for my services." Setting down her goblet, she leaned in to kiss his neck.

"A hefty price indeed," he replied.

"And it isn't something to be learned quickly," she said. "We're going to be spending a lot of time together." She laughed playfully, pulling him in close.

"I intend for us to spend every moment together from now on."

Placing his hands on each side of her head, he unleashed red magic. Paralyzing her with his power, he projected heat through her skull as she screamed in agony. The purple gem hidden in his hand began to glow. Her screams climbed ever higher as he continued to scald her, the heat penetrating deep into her body. After a few moments, she slumped backwards, a flash of purple light filling the amethyst.

Releasing her from his grip, her body rolled lifelessly onto the floor. He gazed inside the gem to see the sparkling light inside take shape. Sirra's face stared back at him, her expression one of torment. With a flick of his fingers, he incinerated her lifeless body, reducing her to nothing more than an insignificant pile of ash.

Chapter 41

About an hour before dawn, Kaiya rose to prepare breakfast for her father and the elves. She still couldn't believe that her mother had gone to town to volunteer as a nurse. Darvil had seemed surprised as well when he informed her of her mother's absence. Kassie rarely ventured to town, even to visit the markets. She took pride in her home, and that is where she spent the vast majority of her time.

Knowing that her elven friends would not eat any meat, Kaiya prepared millet porridge with a touch of honey to sweeten it. Darvil would scoff at such a meal, so she fried some ham and eggs as well. Though she didn't have much practice in the kitchen, she managed to make some biscuits that weren't too flat. They tasted better than they looked, and she knew her father would still enjoy them.

Doozle begged silently at her feet, his brown eyes speaking more loudly than any bark ever could. She gave him a generous helping of ham, which he gobbled up happily. By the time she was finished setting the table, the others had awoken and were ready to eat.

Darvil sat down first. "This looks good," he commented before beginning to eat. The ham was slightly burned, but the eggs were cooked perfectly.

Placing a glass of fresh milk next to her father's plate, Kaiya said, "How does it taste?"

He nodded and grunted in reply, his mouth too full to speak.

River and Galen took their places at the table and tasted the porridge Kaiya had prepared.

"It's good," River said, somewhat surprised. "This would be excellent with almonds."

Kaiya smiled at the compliment. "I'm afraid we don't have any of those." She proceeded to pour him a glass of milk as well, but paused as the bottle touched the cup. "Do you drink milk?"

"No, but I wouldn't mind an ale if you have some," he replied.

"For breakfast?" Darvil said, coughing on his food. "Oh, I like him. He's my kind of elf."

"I'll have ale as well," Galen said, looking to Darvil for his approval.

Darvil nodded, and Kaiya poured ale for each of them before sitting down with her own bowl of porridge. When the meal was finished, Galen jumped to his feet to collect the dishes.

"It's the least I can do," he said. "River gave me another dose of magic, and I have more energy than I need this morning."

"You should still have Lenora take a look at your wound," River suggested. "She will know better than me whether it is healing properly."

Galen shrugged and busied himself washing dishes.

"Does that spell take away from your own strength?" Kaiya asked curiously.

"A bit, but not as much as you would expect," he replied. "The more one practices magic, the larger his or her supply becomes. With elementals, the practice is less necessary. An elemental possesses far larger quantities of magic than the most learned sorcerers."

"I guess your friend on the island found that out," she replied.

"He had a way of draining my power. I've never experienced anything like it. The water restored my magic, but if it wasn't for you, I doubt I would have survived."

"I sensed you were in trouble," she said. "I did what I could. That was the strongest spell I've ever cast, but I didn't feel drained afterward. Shouldn't I have been depleted?"

"You're no ordinary sorcerer, Kaiya," he explained. "The air itself rejuvenates you. As long as you can breathe, your power will not diminish."

"I guess that explains why I've never had the feeling of depleted magic. Why don't all sorcerers study air? It seems like that would be the most beneficial."

"Air is the most difficult element to master," he replied. "And mastering it does not mean that your magical stores will be replenished constantly. There is a difference between an elemental and a sorcerer. Sorcerers replenish their store over time with rest. Elementals are replenished by the element they represent."

Kaiya looked confused. "Are you telling me I'm an elemental?"

"You are unique," he said. "You are wholly a dwarf, but you have immense power. I cannot explain what I do not understand myself."

Kaiya sighed in disappointment. "I hoped you would know more. No one has ever given me a reason for my powers, and I'm starting to think no one ever will."

"Maybe someday," he replied.

"I'll have to find a way to contact an air elemental," she stated with determination. "Surely one of those would know something."

"If I can help you, I will," he promised.

"I, for one, have heard enough talk," Darvil declared, rising to his feet. "There's work to be done around the farm. Give your mother my regards if you run into her in town. Ask her when she's coming home. Dinner doesn't cook itself." He shuffled out the door to tend to his chores.

Kaiya led River and Galen back along the path to the village. The sky was overcast, blocking out a good portion of the sunlight. As they reached the town, Kaiya was surprised to see so many people around. She had feared many more would have taken ill in the four days they had been away. To her relief, there appeared to be more citizens back at work than when she had left.

The medical tent still stood at the far edge of town near the cave. That meant Lenora had not found a cure, but it was obvious her medicine was helping.

"There seems to be a lot of activity around town," River commented, his voice hopeful.

"I noticed that as well," Kaiya replied. "Lenora's doing, no doubt."

The trio continued down the path, making their way to the cave.

"I might as well try to solve the situation now," River said, cradling the opal in his hand.

No sooner had he spoken those words than a loud rumbling rocked the ground beneath his feet. An avalanche of rocks fell violently within the cave entrance, filling the air with a blinding cloud of dust. As the air cleared, it was plain to see that the opening to the cave was completely blocked. Entry was now impossible.

Chapter 42

Gazing into the gem, Telorithan smiled with satisfaction. Sirra's face stared back at him, her hatred for him displayed upon her face. Her entire supply of power was now under his control.

Peering into the amethyst, he said, "I hope you can hear me in there. Is it torment for you?" He laughed at her, adding, "I certainly hope it is. I should have done this before I ever attempted binding the elemental. I could have defeated him easily, as well as his little dwarf pet."

He vowed not to make the same mistake again. He would save Sirra's power in the gem until he was prepared to face a fire elemental. That way, he would guarantee her full strength being added to his own. With more research to do on the lasting power of these gems, he did not want to risk wasting her on any less-important spells. He had wasted the thief's essence when he tossed it in the fire, and he would not do so again with Sirra. Every ounce of magic he could muster would be at his disposal when he was ready to fight again.

As he made his way to the spiral staircase, he paused to admire his reflection in the mirror above the fireplace. There was no sign of his struggle on the island. His face was as pleasing as ever, and he felt pride as he looked upon himself.

I shall have Sirra's gem placed within a crown, he thought. *Once I've achieved my goal, I will need a fitting piece of jewelry.* Laughing again, he shoved the gem into his pocket before proceeding up the stairs.

Arriving at his library, he was determined to find information that would allow him to properly combine Sirra's magic with his own. He could not afford another mistake. With the practice of soul binding being banned, it was difficult to find what he needed. Most Enlightened Elves had their own libraries, but he had no friends willing to allow him access except Yiranor. Yet another visit to his old mentor might be in order.

The University claimed not to carry such texts, but Telorithan knew that to be false. Deep within its archives were tomes and scrolls that were not officially recognized as part of the collection. Even with the practice being outlawed, literature on the subject would not have been destroyed. It was also possible that other masters had stolen these items for safekeeping, or for their own purposes. No member of their race would dare to destroy such valuable texts. There had to be a way to find them.

After hours of scouring his own library, he decided the information he needed was not there. It was a desperate hope that it might be, considering he had already been through every shred of paper within these walls several times before. Originally he feared he had overlooked something, but now he knew there was no other way. He would have to visit the University.

There were several masters there who were former teachers of his. None of them liked him as well as Yiranor did. The elderly master was the only one who ever saw Telorithan as a student worth teaching. The others taught him only to the point of his apprenticeship, and then they turned their backs on him. Once he came under Yiranor's tutelage, he had

309

no need for other teachers. They certainly owed him no favors, but he had ways of getting people to speak.

The idea of torturing some of those elves brought a wicked smile to his lips. They had tortured him during his lessons, and now he might get the chance to return the favor. He was not a forgiving sort of elf, and taking revenge on those he felt had wronged him was a tantalizing thought. He made up his mind to act civilly at first. If his request for access to the archives was refused, they would feel his wrath. Deep down, he hoped they would refuse.

Before heading to the University, he ascended the steps to his bedroom. His servants were not allowed access to this room without him present, so it was the safest place to store the gem containing Sirra's essence. He could not risk having it on his person when he entered the University. If the masters there discovered what he had done, they would jump at the opportunity to imprison him.

There was little chance he could face down all of them. No single one among them could defeat him, but their combined strength would be overwhelming. Recent events had proved that he was not capable of defeating multiple opponents, and he did not yet know how to properly combine Sirra's power to his own.

For now, she would rest safely in a wooden chest with a few other jewels. He gave her one last look before closing the lid. "Soon, dear lady, you shall serve me."

After sealing the room with magic, he descended the stairs to the ground floor of his tower. Exiting onto the street, he was less than thrilled to see that several elves were around. The markets were full of shoppers, and several others seemed to be strolling aimlessly along the path. Everyone seemed to be enjoying the fine weather, courtesy of the air mages who kept a careful watch on any storm systems that were moving in. Some days they succeeded well in their efforts, but other days were too hot. Keeping a semblance of summer year-round was no easy task, and it seemed a most boring profession to Telorithan. When presented with his choice of magic to study, he had chosen fire, knowing he would never be asked to manipulate the weather.

To reach the University, he would need to purchase passage by boat. He lived two islands away from the school, preferring to dwell where the fewest number of elves were present to bother him. Today's crowds were unusual, and he almost wished he could move his tower farther out into the ocean. When he finally achieved his goal of trapping a god, he intended to live a solitary existence. No one would be able to approach his tower without his knowledge, and they would do so at great peril.

The docks were buzzing with activity as well. He took small comfort in the fact that ferries were coming and going more frequently because of the demand. All that meant was more elves were visiting his island than usual. Doing his best to ignore the crowds, he flipped a coin to the ferryman before boarding. He chose a seat at the rear of the vessel and turned his attention to the sea.

Chapter 43

The thunder of crashing boulders attracted a crowd of onlookers to the cave's entrance. River looked at the opal in his hand, knowing it had caused the collapse.

Turning to his companions, he said, "It appears Indal has sensed the magic of the artifact. She knows what's coming."

"It seems she's preparing for a fight," Galen replied.

Kaiya stared at the wall of stone that sealed the entrance. "I never expected her to go quietly. We have to get this cleared away."

Among the crowd was Rudi, the mine foreman. Kaiya approached him boldly, prepared for an argument. He had the men and equipment necessary to clear the entrance, and she was determined to have his help.

He smirked as she neared, knowing what she had in mind. "Don't worry your head about it," he said. "I'll get this cleaned up."

She stood silently a moment, stunned by his willingness to help. "Thank you," she finally remembered to say.

Lenora stepped out of the tent to see the spectacle, but her tired body had other plans. The minute she stepped out into the sunlight, she collapsed to the ground. River saw her from the corner of his eye and rushed to her side, followed by Galen and Kaiya.

As River lifted her into his arms, she opened her eyes and smiled weakly. He carried her inside the tent and placed her gently on an empty cot. Kassie rushed over to see what had happened, a phial of medicine in her hand.

"Has she come down with the same illness as the others?" Galen asked.

"No," Kassie replied. "She's exhausted. She barely sleeps, doesn't eat, and she keeps using her magic to help the sick. Her body isn't cut out for that." She politely pushed River aside to administer some of the medicine to Lenora.

Lenora sat up to take a drink. "I'm fine, really," she insisted.

"You need to rest," Kassie scolded. Looking at River, she added, "Make sure she stays here until she's had a good sleep."

River nodded. "I will." He turned his attention back to Lenora, gently stroking her golden hair.

"You have an important task ahead of you," she whispered. "Don't let me keep you from it."

"The cave entrance is blocked for now," he replied. "I'll stay here with you until it's cleared. Rest now."

"Since we're here," Kaiya began, "let's see about your wound." Leading Galen by the arm, she sat him on a cot and went to fetch her mother.

"Galen is wounded, Mum," she said. "Can you treat him?"

"What kind of wound?" she asked.

"An arrow," Kaiya replied. "We were attacked by Wild Elves."

"Goodness!" Kassie exclaimed. "I never heard such a thing!" She searched through the herbs for one of Lenora's mixtures. Galen would need something to dull the pain and prevent infection. Luckily, Lenora's workstation was kept neat, and Kassie quickly found what she was looking for.

After mixing the herbs in warm water, she brought the concoction to Galen's bedside. "Drink this," she commanded.

After taking a sip, he shuddered. "What's in this?"

"You don't want to know," she replied with a chuckle. "It's better than getting Bron over here, that's for sure." She looked at Kaiya and asked, "Who removed the arrow?"

"I did," Kaiya responded.

Kassie shook her head. "Maybe I should ask Bron to look at it."

"Please," Kaiya replied. "All he wants to do is chop things off or sew them up. I sealed the wound, and River's magic has given him the energy to heal."

"Well, we should still have Lenora take a look," Kassie replied. "You seem to have come back without any scrapes or bruises. I'm happy to see that." She grabbed her daughter and squeezed her tightly. After kissing her on the forehead, she went around the room to check on the other patients.

With the cave's entryway still blocked, there was little for Kaiya to do but wait. She kept her mother company while Lenora and Galen rested. River sat vigil next to Lenora. As she slept soundly, he placed a hand on the side of her head. Blue magic spread through her body, giving her a small amount of power to rejuvenate her. It was the same spell he used on Galen, and he hoped it would take away some of her exhaustion.

Lenora awoke, her pale eyes sparkling. "I feel much better," she said. She sat up on her cot, despite River's protests.

"You should continue to rest," he said.

"I'm fine," she insisted, getting to her feet. "I have something for you." She walked over to her desk to find the ring Ortin had crafted for her.

Kassie gave her a stern look. "Back to bed with you!" she insisted.

Lenora nodded and headed back to her cot. Taking a seat, she presented the ring to River. The band was made of shining silver, and a sapphire stone was set in the middle. "I had this crafted for you," she said.

Taking the ring, River immediately placed it on his finger. "It's beautiful," he said, looking into her eyes. "I thank you for this gift, and I shall wear it always." Placing a hand on her face, he leaned in to kiss her soft pink lips. "I'm afraid I have nothing to give you," he said.

"You've returned safely," she replied. "That's all I could ever ask for." She paused for a moment and added, "I love you, River."

With a smile, he replied, "And I love you, Lenora." He leaned in for a second kiss, this one lasting longer than the first. Lenora lay back on her cot, intending to get some more rest. Kassie was staring at them, and the last thing Lenora wanted was for her to come over and scold her for not sleeping.

Kaiya smiled, happy to see the two of them together. She could tell there was a special bond between them, and she hoped they would make each other happy for many long years to come. Glancing over at Galen, she could see that he had slept through everything. She sighed softly to herself.

After a few hours, Rudi entered the tent to tell them the cave entrance had been cleared. It was time to see if the artifact still held the power needed to release Indal.

Chapter 44

River stood, taking one last look at Lenora's sleeping form. He hesitated before exiting the tent, remembering Ryllak's words. "Never be too proud to ask for help," his father had said. Originally, he had believed this was a task he would perform alone. However, Kaiya's presence had saved him from Telorithan, and her powers were growing ever stronger. She may well be the difference between success and failure.

Approaching Kaiya and her mother, he said, "Kaiya, would you be willing to help me?"

Jumping to her feet, she replied, "Of course."

"Your assistance is most appreciated," he said with sincerity.

Kassie looked worried. "Be careful, both of you," she said, her voice shaking. The thought of her daughter going in there with a dangerous entity was difficult to digest. Indal had brought those rocks crashing down, and she could do so again with Kaiya inside.

Kaiya gently touched her mother's shoulder. "We'll be fine, Mum. I promise." She felt certain that she and River would succeed. If it cost her life, it was a small price to pay to rid her people of a terrible fate.

Side by side, they walked to the cave's entrance. The sun was setting, and darkness was descending upon the village. A few dwarves looked up as the pair walked by, but none of them uttered a word.

Together they entered the cave, the foreboding presence of Indal still heavy in the air. The ground shook as they neared the pool where her spirit resided, and they took great care with each step. River held the opal firmly in his hand, his mind focused on subduing Indal.

"I hope this works," Kaiya commented. River did not reply.

As they neared the pool, Indal's form began to glow, taking shape above the water. Knowing what the elf carried with him made her tense, and her expression was severe.

"You will not defeat me!" she cried, her voice echoing from the stone walls.

Kaiya and River stepped forth, showing no fear. River raised the opal high above his head, all of his energy focused into it. Kaiya created a shield to protect them both in case Indal was still able to attack.

Indal was aware of the danger. Mustering every bit of energy available to her, she pulled power from the cave itself. Blasts of energy emitted from her form as she desperately tried to stop them from performing the ancient ritual. She could feel Nicodun's energy within the stone, his immense power having left a permanent mark upon it. Her hatred for her former lover only heightened her desire to remain in the cave.

Kaiya readied herself for the attack, determined to protect herself and River from Indal's energy blast. With both palms outstretched, she steeled herself against the magic hurtling toward her. Her entire focus poured into the shield, and the blast bounced off, returning to the caster. Indal was unfazed, her body absorbing the energy as it struck her.

As River continued to concentrate on the stone, a white light surrounded his hands. His mind was focused only on freeing Indal's trapped spirit, in hopes that she would cross over in peace. Her wrath was caused by her capture, and freedom, he hoped, would mean an end to her torment.

The light continued to grow, forming into a beam that locked onto Indal's glowing form.

"You will never be rid of me!" she cried. "I will never leave this place!"

The beam held steady for a moment while Indal continued to mutter as if the stone were speaking with her. Neither Kaiya nor River heard any voice from the stone, but Indal's desperate cries were plain to their ears. The beam grew more intense, forcing Kaiya to shield her eyes. Her shield faltered momentarily, but she quickly refocused her mind to maintaining its strength.

With a piercing shriek, the beam intensified, centering itself on Indal. In an instant, her form shattered, exploding into dust before their eyes. The blast hit Kaiya's shield, and she needed all of her physical strength to hold it steady. The opal in River's hands continued to glow until it too burst into pieces. River fell to his knees, exhausted from the effort.

Dropping the shield, Kaiya reached out for him. "Are you hurt?" she asked.

He shook his head. "Do you sense Indal?"

Kaiya looked around the cave, wondering if Indal was still around. "I sense nothing," she replied. "Did she cross over?"

"No," he replied quietly. "She was destroyed." He looked at his hands, which had once held the artifact. The reality of his actions had not yet set in. Though he had hoped to free her from her torment and allow her to pass into the afterlife, he had instead destroyed her completely.

"I failed," he said, burying his head in his hands.

"No," Kaiya replied. "You have saved my people. She would never have stopped tormenting them, and many more would have died as her anger continued."

"I killed her," he whispered.

"She chose death," Kaiya said, hoping to ease his mind. "The stone gave her a choice, and she refused to go. There's nothing more you could do for her. The torment she felt living here is over, at least."

River said nothing but slowly rose back to his feet. Kaiya took his hand to lead him from the cave. They walked slowly through the darkness until the moonlight appeared before them.

"I must speak to the Spirit," River said quietly as they stepped outside the cave. He left her side without another word, slowly heading for the stream at the far edge of town.

Kaiya watched as he walked away, still concerned for her friend. He was clearly upset by what had happened, and she did not know how else to console him. She did not blame him for Indal's destruction. That was clearly the path Indal had chosen. The dwarves were now safe, thanks to River. He was a hero, not a murderer. Kaiya hoped that in time he would realize that.

Chapter 45

To his surprise, Telorithan was granted full access to the University archives without encountering any sort of opposition. For several hours, he scoured the shelves for even the tiniest hint at information regarding soul binding. Eventually, his eyes fell on a tattered tome. It nearly crumbled at his grasp, and several of the pages were loose. The title revealed unmistakably what the book was about: *Binding the Essence.*

Nearly salivating at this discovery, he quickly found a seat far from the other elves who were present in the library. With great delicacy, he turned the pages of the old volume. The majority of the book was unreadable, it's advanced age and lack of care being evident. For a moment, he contemplated inquiring if there was a second copy available, but he knew that question would only lead to trouble.

What he could make out defined the process in great detail. Illustrations depicted adding the essence of a creature to a weapon, thereby enhancing its abilities. To his dismay, there was no mention of adding another person's essence to one's own. If this tome had contained the information, it had long since succumbed to time.

Telorithan took a closer look at the section describing weapons enhancement. A simple spell was all that was needed once the essence had been extracted. After having the gem inlaid in the strongest part of the weapon, one needed only to cast a second binding spell in order to meld the power to the weapon.

Could such a thing be possible with a person? He wondered how he might go about inlaying a gem into himself. The idea seemed silly. *I am no mere object*, he thought. *There must be another way.*

As he once again turned to the front of the book, he decided to check each page intently. Three-quarters into the volume, he found something that he had missed before.

"A sorcerer's essence may be extracted at the moment of death if he desires eternal life. Only his most trusted apprentice should have access to the gem, which he must have placed in a setting to keep near him at all times. A ring or necklace is often preferred, and the wearer is given the option of having the excess power on hand at all times...[illegible text]...combines with that of the apprentice, forming a permanent bond."

Surprised, Telorithan looked up from his reading. Could there truly be nothing necessary other than having the gem at his side? This text would suggest that whoever held the gem controlled the power inside. He marveled at the simplicity and at the author's lack of knowledge. Suggesting this process as a path to immortality was an error. The elf within the gem lived on in torment, which was a major factor in banning the practice. This text was obviously written before that bit of information was uncovered. Telorithan laughed quietly to himself, wondering if the book's author had subjected himself to it in hopes of living forever.

Content that he had found the information he needed, Telorithan returned the tome to the shelves. All he needed to do was retrieve his gem and set it into a piece of jewelry. He could not possibly hand the amethyst over to a jeweler, so he would have to manage that part himself. He could purchase an empty setting and place the gem inside it. Then, he would take some time to practice casting spells with Sirra's magic combined with his own. If he was successful, he would be ready to face the elemental far sooner than anticipated. There would be no need to wait years, as he had feared.

With hurried feet, he made his way back to the docks to return to his own island. There were several jewelers in the market district. Surely, one of them would have what he required. He took a seat and waited impatiently for the boat to carry him back home. There was a smaller crowd than before, as night was quickly falling over the isles.

Stepping off the ferry, he practically ran to the market area. Several of the shops had already closed, but to his relief, one jewelry shop remained open. His eyes skimmed over the assortment of rings until he found one that seemed large enough to hold Sirra's amethyst.

"This one," he said to the young elf behind the counter.

The red-haired elf startled at the sound of the sorcerer's voice. Telorithan was known to him through reputation, and he had hoped the elf would leave without speaking to him. He was frightened of the sorcerer, and he was doing a poor job hiding it. Stumbling forward, he opened the case and lifted the ring for Telorithan to try on.

Slipping it onto his right forefinger, Telorithan admired the ring. It was a large emerald set in ornately wrought silver. The ring showed signs of advanced age, which only made him like it more. There was obviously a history behind this piece of jewelry.

"I'll take it," he said. "Remove the emerald."

The young elf stared at him, obviously confused.

"Are you deaf?" he asked. "Remove the stone. I require only the setting."

"Forgive me," the elf said, stumbling. "My master would be furious. The price is for the ring with the stone."

"I'm not here to argue the price," the sorcerer replied. "I will pay for both pieces, but you will remove the stone for me."

The young elf swallowed hard and nodded. He turned quickly to his workbench and removed the stone from the ring. Handing it over to Telorithan, he asked, "Will there be anything else?"

Tossing a bag of coins onto the counter, he replied, "No." He stuck the emerald in his pocket and placed the empty ring on his finger. *This will look fantastic on me*, he thought. His mind swirling with possibilities, he returned to his tower to set the amethyst into his new ring. It wouldn't be long before he would fully control Sirra's power. With her magic added to his, he would be unstoppable.

Chapter 46

After spending a restless night at the water's edge, River could see light finally beginning to appear in the sky. He waded down into the stream, hoping the Spirit would come to him. His heart weighed heavily over the loss of Indal, and he was unsure if he had made the correct decision in using the opal.

Sliding down into the water, River turned his thoughts to the Spirit. He heard only the sound of water until a voice came into his mind.

Indal's torment is at an end.

"She has been destroyed," River replied. "Her essence is lost forever."

Her torment has ended, the spirit repeated. *You set out to free her, and you have done so.*

"That does little to ease my mind," he replied. "She has been lost by my hand. That is not the remedy I had hoped for."

She chose her own destruction. Think on her no more.

River opened his eyes, feeling that the Spirit had departed. It had offered him little comfort, and he still did not know if he had made the right decision to use the opal against her. His intention was to free her from her bonds, but he did not mean to destroy her entirely. He had hoped she would enjoy peace in the afterlife, but it was not to be.

As the sun moved higher in the sky, he slowly made his way back to the village. Kaiya was waiting for him near the markets. When he finally came into view, she smiled cheerfully and waved. She could see that he still felt burdened, and she hoped to relieve some of his guilt.

"The dwarves that were still in the hospital are all leaving. Every one of them is cured," she said.

"That is good to know," he replied, his voice still troubled.

Kaiya took his hand and placed the remnants of the opal in his palm. "I salvaged what I could," she said. "Maybe you can learn more about the artifact in time. There could still be a way to help Indal."

River looked upon her with kindness. The Spirit's words were final, and he knew there would be no further help for Indal. However, he did not wish to burden Kaiya with that information. "Thank you, my friend," he said, closing his fingers around the shattered pieces. The opal was useless now, its magic having been fully spent. The gem would never be whole again, and it would never possess the power it once held.

Opening his hand to look upon the remains, he realized how beautiful the stones still were. Perhaps they could have another use after all. It would be a shame to dispose of the ancient stone fragments. "Where can I find Ortin? I'd like to have a gift made for Lenora."

"He has a stall here in the marketplace," Kaiya replied, pointing. She led him to the smith's shop.

The black-bearded dwarf smiled happily as River and Kaiya approached. He gripped River's hand in a firm shake and said, "I can't thank you enough. You've saved us all from that witch in the cave."

River smiled politely. "Her curse has ended," he replied. Looking at Kaiya, he added, "Kaiya played an important role as well."

"She's a fine girl," he stated, nodding to her. "What brings you two to see me?"

River showed the opal fragments to the smith. "Could you fashion one of these into a ring for Lenora? Something delicate would be nice."

Ortin took the fragments from him and inspected them closely. "I'll need a few hours to shape the stone properly, but I'd be more than happy to help. I would surely have died if not for Lenora. She'll have the prettiest ring you ever saw." The smith turned and immediately searched through his tools.

"We'll be back later," Kaiya said, ushering River from the shop.

In a stall nearby, Galen had found his way back to work with Trin. "Hello there," he said as he saw his friends approaching.

"You're all better, it seems," River replied.

"Yes," Galen said. "I thought I'd try to learn a few more things about these runes before they kick us out of here."

"You'll always be welcome here," Kaiya replied, a sadness coming over her. She had no desire for the elves to leave, especially Galen. Over the last few days, she had grown fond of him, and she had never known true friendship before.

"They're planning a feast of celebration tonight at the council house. I suspect they want to give River a medal." Galen winked at Kaiya, hoping to at least get a smile in return. Her expression remained cheerless, which worried him. "Not even a little smile?" he said with a grin. "I'll have to see what I can do about that," he declared. "I'll have you grinning ear to ear before long. Mark my words."

Kaiya smiled half-heartedly. She did not wish to spoil his good mood, but she was dreading the thought of being alone once again. Having other people around who were familiar with magic was nice. It was also nice to have friends. Her parents loved her dearly, but they could not fill all the lonely places in her heart.

River was anxious to visit with Lenora. Leaving Kaiya behind with Galen, he hurried to the hospital tent. To his surprise, the dwarves were already dismantling it. Lenora's face lit up at the sight of him.

"They're all cured, every one of them," she said happily. "You saved them."

"You saved them first," he replied. "More would have lost their lives had you not been here to treat them."

"I did what I could," she said. "I'll admit I used a lot of the herbs the dryads taught me about. I owe them my gratitude, and I still have much left to learn from them." Her voice was full of hope and a touch of excitement.

"Do you plan to continue living among the dryads?" he asked, hoping that was not her intention. He wanted her to stay in the Vale and be at his side forever.

"Maybe," she replied. "I haven't really had time to think about it." She took his arm and followed him to a nearby bench. "What happened in the cave? Did you free Indal?"

River hung his head. Quietly, he replied, "She was destroyed. She refused freedom."

Lenora could see the sadness in his eyes. Laying her hand on the side of his face, she said, "You have done a great thing for these people. Indal had turned into a creature of pure evil, and she would never have stopped plaguing them. Please, take comfort in knowing these dwarves owe you their lives. Indal is no longer in pain, and her hatred can't hurt anyone else."

Though Kaiya and the Spirit had both made similar statements, hearing it from his love gave it more meaning. How could he ever feel sad with her around? Gently, he kissed her lips and embraced her tightly. "I love you, Lenora," he said, looking into her pale eyes.

Though he would never forget Indal's fate, his guilt would subside with time. As the dwarf people continued to prosper, and new generations were born, he could take comfort in knowing he had helped make their lives possible. The plague was at an end.

Chapter 47

The dwarves busied themselves setting up tables and preparing food for the evening celebration. With everyone feeling better, they were eager for some revelry. Days of lying in bed with fever were now behind them, and a party would help lift their spirits once again.

Anid stood on the porch of the council house, trying to manage the crowd. Nearly everyone in town had shown up to join in the festivities, and the ale had been flowing freely since early afternoon. Some of them were already stumbling.

"Your attention, please!" Anid called over the noise of the crowd. Hardly anyone acknowledged his presence.

Looking defeated, he motioned to Kaiya. "Can you do anything about this?" he asked, a twinkle in his eye.

With a nod, she closed her eyes and focused energy into her fingertips. Sparks danced from her fingers, and she shot them into the air. With a pop and a fizzle, they attracted the attention of the feasting dwarves. Many of them looked to the sky in awe.

"Thank you," Anid said. To the crowd he announced, "We have gathered tonight to celebrate our friendship with the elves of the Vale, River and Galen. Together with one of our own," he motioned to Kaiya, "they have secured an end to the evil plague that befell us. We are in your debt."

The crowd applauded, lifting their mugs to toast their heroes. Kaiya felt slightly embarrassed. She had never fit in among the villagers, and she had certainly never had cause to celebrate among them.

"Drink up," Galen said, handing her a frothy mug.

She accepted the drink, and raised it high. "To friendship," she said.

River snuck away from the party momentarily to meet with Ortin. He had already completed the ring, having secured the opal in a silver setting. Proudly, the smith presented it to River.

"Some of my finest work ever," he declared.

"I am in your debt," River replied.

Ortin shook his head. "Think nothing of it. Lenora deserves all the finest."

With a few butterflies in his stomach, River approached Lenora. She turned to smile at him, a mug of ale in her delicate hand.

"I have a gift for you," he said, taking her hand. He placed the ring on her finger before kissing the back of her hand.

"It's lovely," she said. "Thank you." Setting down her mug, she wrapped her arms tightly around him and kissed his cheek. "I shall treasure it to my last day," she declared.

Galen and Kaiya witnessed their embrace and moved in to join them. They hugged each other in turn, Lenora and Kaiya hugging the longest.

"I'm going to miss you," Lenora said. "I didn't get to know you as well as I would have liked, but you feel almost like a sister to me. I hope we will meet again."

Kaiya nodded, tears spilling from her eyes. "I hope so too."

"Okay," Galen said. "Now that everyone's crying, I have an announcement to make."

The three stared at him, waiting for him to continue. He hesitated, hoping to create a dramatic effect. Raised eyebrows were his friends' only response.

"I'm staying here," he said.

Kaiya felt as if she might faint. "You mean it?" she asked.

"Yes," he replied. "I want to study with Trin, and I'm not ready to leave the friends I've made here." He smiled at her, and she felt herself blush.

Her eyes filling with tears for the second time, Kaiya stepped forward to embrace Galen. They held each other tightly for a moment, while River and Lenora looked on. Their faces beamed with happiness for their friends.

"I think it's about time we were heading home," River declared. "Our job here is finished."

"Another staircase made of water?" Lenora asked, a note of mischief in her voice.

"I had something a little more fun in mind," he replied with a grin.

"Never give ale to a water elemental," Galen said in jest.

The four of them proceeded down the path that would lead them back to the waterfall. The stars were appearing in the sky, their light reflecting on the river below.

"I'll miss you both," Kaiya said. "Maybe we can talk more about getting in touch with an air elemental." She hugged each of them again before saying, "Goodbye, my friends." Taking Galen's hand, she knew her life was about to change for the better.

River grabbed Lenora in his arms. "Ready?" he asked.

"For wh—" she started to say. Before she knew what was happening, she was sliding down the waterfall as it rushed toward the Vale. Despite her trust in River, she cried out in fear, her voice echoing as they descended from the mountain. With a splash, they landed in the pool beneath, River's arms still secured around her waist.

"That wasn't so bad, was it?" he asked playfully.

She shook her head. Her cry had brought spectators from the elven village to investigate the sound. Ryllak was first among them. He had kept a vigil over the waterfall since returning to the Vale, hoping every day that his son would return.

As River and Lenora stepped onto the bank, Ryllak grabbed his son and squeezed him tightly. "It's good to have you back," he said, his relief obvious on his face. His son had never been away before, and he was glad to see him unharmed.

Myla and Albyn were not nearly so happy. Seeing their daughter locked in River's embrace did not sit well with either of them. Still, they were glad to see Lenora home safely, and they greeted her warmly.

Myla noticed the ring on Lenora's finger. "Did the dwarves give you that?" she asked, already knowing what Lenora would say.

"They crafted it, but it was a gift from River," she replied. "I love him." Turning away from her parents, she rejoined River. Slipping her arm in his, they walked together under the moonlight, ignoring the rest of the world. This night they would spend together.

Chapter 48

Y iranor was surprised to hear that Telorithan was waiting for him in the sitting room. He had not expected there to be any new developments in his former student's soul binding research so quickly. Perhaps he had more questions, but Yiranor had already given him every bit of information he had on the subject. He doubted the visit was merely a social call. Telorithan wasn't the sort of elf who enjoyed company.

Telorithan tapped a finger on the arm of his chair as he waited for his former mentor to meet him. He had no intention of telling him about his recent failures. Only Sirra had knowledge of the mess he had made with Koru's binding, and he had told no one else of his encounter with River. His eyes narrowed as he peered into his ring, wondering if Sirra might have the ability to mock him in her current state. *Nonsense,* he thought. *I control her essence. She no longer has any free will.*

Finally, Yiranor made his appearance, a warm expression on his face. "Welcome back," he said. "What brings you to see me again so soon?"

"I'm heading to the Red Isle," he replied. "I've come to see if you have thought of anything else I need to know."

Yiranor's eyes went wide, as he was visibly taken aback. "Already?" he asked. "You're going to attempt binding an elemental?" He couldn't believe his former pupil could have perfected his technique in so short a time.

"I have augmented my own supply of power. There is no use in waiting any longer." His expression was smug and self-assured. With Sirra, he knew he would not fail again.

"I have searched my library most thoroughly, I assure you," the old elf said. "I have found no further information that could assist you." He stared openly at Telorithan, still dumbfounded by his announcement.

Telorithan stood. "I suppose I'll be off, then."

Before he could leave, Yiranor remembered something that might help. "Wait, please," he said. "I have an item which might prove useful. Give me a moment to retrieve it." Gesturing with his hand, he implored the silver-haired sorcerer to sit down.

Telorithan obeyed with a sigh. Whatever the old master had in mind had better be worth the delay. It was clear he had learned nothing new, and Telorithan was now eager to leave.

After a few minutes, Yiranor returned with a jeweled cuff in his hand. "This is an heirloom of my house," he explained. "Take this. It is said to contain immense power." As he handed the cuff to his student, he caught a glimpse of the purple stone on his forefinger. Inside was the unmistakable visage of Sirra, her form trapped forever in a swirling silver mist.

Yiranor drew in a breath quickly at the sight. Staring only a moment, he looked away before Telorithan could notice his shocked expression. He understood how Telorithan had come by the power to face an elemental so quickly. Taking the essence of the thief had been a small matter, but binding the soul of a dear and trusted friend was another thing entirely. Yiranor shuddered at the thought. It could easily have been him in that ring.

Taking the cuff from his former mentor, Telorithan turned it over in his hand. He could feel magic radiating from it. Its edges were embellished with runes, and four rubies glowed brightly upon it.

"This is a generous gift," he said.

"I have no sons of my own to give it to," Yiranor replied. "I hope you will use it well." For an instant, he wondered if giving him the cuff sooner would have saved Sirra's life. He knew better, however. If Telorithan could accumulate different sources of power, he would take them no matter the price. Sirra sealed her fate by getting too close to him. Yiranor hoped that Telorithan would succeed in his quest, and leave him in peace thereafter. He both loved and feared his former student. Telorithan was capable of almost anything, and there was little help for those who stood in his path.

"We shall meet again," Telorithan said as he stood near the door. "Once I've bound one of his minions, I will require further research before challenging Yelaurad."

"You are traveling today?" Yiranor asked.

"This very moment," he replied before exiting.

Yiranor was relieved to have his guest depart. Still, part of him yearned to see Telorithan succeed. No elf in history had accomplished what his pupil was setting out to do. He marveled at the power Telorithan might possess at their next encounter. If more research were in order, Yiranor would begin now. Staying in the sorcerer's good graces was his only chance of avoiding his anger.

Telorithan found himself once again at the docks, where he had already arranged private passage to the Red Isle. Few elves traveled there, and the ones who did were normally students. There would be no other ships bound for the same destination on this day. He made sure of that using a bag of gold and gems. Today was for him alone, and he would not have any interruptions.

Slipping the cuff onto his wrist, he could feel its warmth against his flesh. It was truly a thing of beauty, and he respected Yiranor for gifting it to him. Perhaps it would be the tipping point to success should his encounter prove more difficult than anticipated. The item was clearly ancient, created in a time when the Enlightened Elves held true power. Now, they were servants of the University and the Grand Council. They had given up raw elemental power in exchange for a pathetic civilization. The elves willingly limited their own power for the sake of adhering to the rules.

Telorithan had always disagreed with such nonsense. A sorcerer's power should be inhibited by nothing.

Without a word to the crewmen, he boarded the small vessel that would bear him to his destiny. A force was pulling at him, willing him to complete his mission. It was almost as if a voice were saying, "Come and claim me. I am yours!" Every elemental on the isle would tremble before him, and he would choose the strongest for his opponent. Today, he would meet his destiny.

Chapter 49

Life in the dwarf village returned to normal for the most part. The only thing that remained out of the ordinary was Galen's presence. He was likable and friendly, and most of the dwarves took to him readily. He was settling in nicely and eager to learn all he could. For the first time, he felt like he belonged. Not only had he found a profession that suited him, he had found where his heart truly longed to be. Having Kaiya nearby was an added bonus.

Kaiya returned to the farmhouse with her mother. Kassie was no longer needed as a nurse, and she was content to return to the farm and her knitting. Kaiya loved living on the farm, and she could not see herself moving to the village in the near future. The citizens had been much more friendly to her since the evil presence had been vanquished, but Kaiya still didn't feel comfortable around them. Too many years as an outcast had taken its toll, and she was happier staying away from the village most days.

Galen had promised to visit often, and she would be willing to spend time in town to enjoy his company. Today, she sat behind her favorite tree, listening closely to the wind. Sparks danced on her fingertips as she playfully moved her hand along the breeze. Deep inside, new powers had been unlocked during her journey. Her desperate desire to help a friend had opened up a new world of possibilities. She could feel her powers growing stronger, and it was exhilarating, as well as frightening. Someday she hoped to visit the Vale and learn from the scholars who lived there. One of them might be able to help her develop her gift properly. For now she would continue to practice, learning only from the wind itself.

As night descended, Kaiya went inside. She was glad to have her mother at home to cook. Darvil's cooking was less than edible, and Kaiya's kitchen skills left much to be desired. Kassie enjoyed feeding her family, and she took pride in her cooking.

Before beginning his meal, Darvil said, "I still wish you'd find a husband. Someone out there will have to look after you when I'm gone."

"I can look after myself," she replied, feeling as if she'd had this conversation a million times. "My magic is stronger now. I'm in a better position to protect my future husband, should I choose to take one." Her thoughts turned to Galen and whether they might one day be wed. Neither culture had any precedent of marriage between them.

Shaking her head, she put the thought away. The two certainly had feelings for each other, but whether it would turn into something more than friendship she could not be sure. Galen was too quick to make jokes, and getting him to be serious and discuss something so important might prove impossible. Still, she hoped to have such a conversation in the near future. Her heart leapt at the sight of him, and she suspected he might have a similar feeling upon seeing her.

"My precious girl can take care of herself and her husband," Kassie said, taking her seat. "There's a handsome elf in the village who's been keeping a close eye on her." She smiled knowingly at her daughter.

Kaiya blushed. Had her feelings been so plain to see? Her mother always knew what she was feeling, and it was difficult to keep secrets from her.

"Elf?" Darvil asked, his brow ruffled. "I never heard of such a thing," he scoffed. "An elf and a dwarf." He took a bite of food and chewed it thoughtfully. After a moment of silence, he added, "I guess that wouldn't be so bad."

Kaiya couldn't help but smile at his words. Darvil had made it clear that he would be highly selective about the man she might choose to wed, and having his approval meant a lot to her. She and Kassie exchanged looks, both trying to contain their joy.

* * * * *

River and Lenora spent a pleasant evening together beneath the stars. Seeking privacy behind the waterfall, River carried Lenora through the water to keep her dry.

As he placed her on a large stone, she asked, "How is it you can come out of the water without a drop on you?"

He shrugged and raised his eyebrows. "It's an elemental thing, I suppose."

Sitting by her side, he placed his arm around her shoulders. The sound of the rushing waterfall filled the air, and fireflies glowed on and off above the flowing water.

"Lenora," River said. "Would you consider becoming my life-mate?" His sapphire eyes looked into hers. He knew he would never desire another woman, nor would his love for her ever diminish. She was everything he could ever wish for, and he hoped to join with her forever.

"Yes," she replied. "But not yet."

He looked at her questioningly. "When?" he asked.

"I have much still to learn, and I would like to travel as well." She paused for a moment and looked away. "You could come with me."

"I may leave the Vale only with the Spirit's consent. I doubt I could be away for long." He bowed his head, sorrow overcoming him.

Lenora placed a hand on his cheek and said softly, "I love you, and I will be your life-mate someday. There are other cultures where I can learn medicine. There is knowledge that has been lost to our people who are blessed with such resilient health. Other races are not so lucky. I might have saved more dwarves if I had more knowledge."

"I understand," River replied. "I'll be waiting for you when you return."

"I'm not leaving yet," she said with a smile. She snuggled up next to him and rested her head on his shoulder. "Tell me," she said. "Can you see my future?"

River smiled and remained silent.

Chapter 50

Telorithan stepped onto the barren wasteland that was the Red Isle. Taking in a deep breath, his lungs filled with hot air and ash. The ground beneath his feet quaked as the volcano spewed forth an orange river of lava. The island was alive with fire, and he could sense the presence of many elementals.

Yelaurad himself was said to have taken up residence inside the volcano. The Sunswept Isles experienced many earthquakes and tremors, thanks to his presence. He was a wrathful god who did not like to be forgotten. His rumblings were a constant reminder of his continued presence among the Enlightened Elves. Though they no longer worshiped the old gods, they revered them as beings of pure magic. The true nature of the gods was not fully understood.

The sorcerer toyed with his ring momentarily, twisting it back and forth upon his finger. He looked into the dull eyes of Sirra, hoping she would provide enough power to tip the scales in his favor. The jeweled cuff on his wrist was already buzzing with energy, sensing the presence of raw, untamed magical power.

Keeping his distance from the volcano, Telorithan intended to find an elemental on the side of the island that sat nearest to the rest of the Sunswept Isles. It was far too dangerous to approach the volcano, and the concentration of power there would be overwhelming in his current state. Elementals were in good supply all over this island, and he intended to challenge one in single combat.

The water elemental had no honor, he mused. *It brought along a friend for help.* With a deep breath, he put his thoughts of River and Kaiya aside. Anger would not help him in his endeavor. He needed a clear mind and the ability to focus if he wished to succeed. His revenge would have to wait a while.

Spotting a smaller magma flow that was slowly creeping away from its source, Telorithan decided on his target. There was clearly an elemental within this flow, and it would serve his purpose well.

Striding forth to challenge his opponent, he approached the flow with confidence. "I am Telorithan, master of fire. I challenge you to combat."

There was no reply other than the continued sputtering of the volcano, and the gentle roar of the ocean. Refusing to become angry, the sorcerer reached into his pocket and retrieved a large, flawless ruby.

He held the gemstone in front of him and declared, "This shall be your resting place! I summon you from your fiery home. Face me, coward!"

The ruby's presence caught the attention of the nearby elemental. It knew Telorithan's purpose, and it would be forced to defend itself. To do otherwise would be risking eternal torment. It took on a humanoid shape, rising to a height of nine feet and wearing a shield of lava.

Telorithan took a step back, awed by the form of the elemental. It was a beautiful sight, which he beheld with envy. His own beauty paled by comparison. Here was a creature of pure fire, and he lusted to possess it. Not only would he bind its essence, but he also would combine it with his own, intertwining their powers for all time.

Mustering all of his strength, Telorithan struck first. His hands radiated with red energy as he lifted them toward the elemental. Throwing blast after blast, he hoped to weaken it before tapping into his newest resources.

The elemental roared as it was bombarded with wave after wave of energy. It became furious, its red coat bursting into flame. Moving forward, it shot fire at its attacker, but the sorcerer was prepared. He protected himself with a green earthen shield, courtesy of Sirra's magic.

Telorithan held fast against the elemental's constant barrage of attacks. Sirra obviously possessed more power than he had realized. Keeping his mind clear, he tapped into the power supply of the cuff. With its added strength, he created a blast powerful enough to knock the elemental off-balance and send it tumbling among the ash.

Once the elemental was down, Telorithan knew success was at hand. With a deep breath, he reached inside for his last ounce of strength. Using the combined powers of earth and fire, he sealed the elemental in a web of magic. He drained its power as it writhed and kicked in agony.

Telorithan's excitement grew as he felt the elemental's raw power enter his body. This was far more thrilling than his previous attempt on the water elemental. Water was nothing. Fire was his true nature, and he would have it.

Drained and weak, the elemental could no longer defend against his attack. With a smile of triumph, he reached forth to remove its essence. A beam of red light emitted from the creature's heart, despite its feeble attempts to squirm free. The beam only intensified as it fell upon the ruby in the sorcerer's hand. With a blast of light, the form of the elemental disappeared before his eyes. In its place was only a burned shape upon the sand.

Nearly overcome with pride, Telorithan gazed inside the ruby. It was hot to the touch, and it burned his skin to hold it. A burn was a small matter, and he found he enjoyed the sensation more and more as he continued to squeeze the gem in his hand.

"I shall be a god!" he cried, turning to face the volcano. Lifting the gem high in the air, it reflected the orange light spewing forth from the caldera. It was an intoxicating feeling that Telorithan had craved for so long. Now the power was his, and he had only one step to complete: combining his own essence with the one trapped inside the ruby.

Far away in the Vale, River felt a sudden sensation of heat. Looking toward the ocean, he shuddered. The natural balance of the world had been disturbed. An elemental had been defeated.

About the Author

Lana Axe lives in Missouri near the edge of the woods. She is inspired by her love of nature to write about elves, magic and adventure. Growing up in Mark Twain's backyard inspired her love of fiction from an early age. She grew up an avid reader and went on to study literature in college.

For more information, please visit: lana-axe.com

Made in the USA
Lexington, KY
05 May 2014